FOOTSTEPS IN THE PARK
Marie Joseph

Marie Joseph was born in Lancashire and was educated at Blackburn High School for Girls. Until her marriage she was in the Civil Service.

She now lives in Middlesex with her husband, a Chartered Engineer, and they have two married daughters.

After a very successful career as a short story writer, Marie Joseph now writes novels set in her native Lancashire, in periods ranging from the turn of the century to the present time. No less than four of her novels have been short-listed for the Romantic Novelist's Association Award during the past few years. She is a well-known public speaker and broadcasts frequently on Radio Four and the Overseas Programmes.

Marie Joseph is also the author of ONE STEP AT A TIME, the moving and at times hilarious account of her constant battle against Rheumatoid Arthritis.

Footsteps in the Park

MARIE JOSEPH

ARROW BOOKS

Arrow Books Limited
17-21 Conway Street, London W1P 6JD

An imprint of the Hutchinson Publishing Group

London Melbourne Sydney Auckland
Johannesburg and agencies throughout
the world

First published by Macdonald & Jane's 1978
Arrow edition 1982

Set in Linoterm Baskerville by
Book Economy Services, Crawley, Sussex

Made and printed in Great Britain
by the Anchor Press Ltd
Tiptree, Essex

ISBN 0 09 930000 1

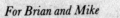

For Brian and Mike

One

Stanley was late, and it wasn't like him. Usually he was there before her.

'Same time, same place,' he'd said the day before after they'd said their lingering goodbyes at the Corporation Park gates, and Dorothy had watched him walk away from her, dark head bent, as if his addiction to study had weakened his neck muscles, planting his undeniably big feet awkwardly as if he were counting the cracks in the pavement.

Although it was nearly May, and supposed to be spring, there was a sad soft drizzle in the air, and a sighing wind shivered the branches of the surrounding trees into nebulous shapes. Dorothy shivered and pulled the collar of her navy-blue gaberdine raincoat up round her neck, sinking herself further down into it and moving to the far end of the park bench.

She met Stanley Armstrong every day, after school finished at four o'clock, to sit close to him in innocent proximity, partially hidden from passers-by by rhododendron bushes and a weeping willow tree, oblivious to anything but their all-consuming and fascinated interest in each other.

At that time of day, little groups of men, some of whom had been on the dole for long periods since coming home from France in 1918, were making their way home. Shuffling along the paths of the town's Corporation Park in twos and threes, smoking their Woodbines down to the last fraction of an inch, making their way back to their terraced houses in the narrow winding streets. Flat-capped and morose, with scarves knotted carelessly over collarless shirts made of striped union flannel.

The Lancashire town, in the depths of the early thirties depression, was a standing on corners, holding its breath kind of place, with the ache of idleness stamped on the faces of its menfolk. The disparity between those who had and those who had not as great as at any time in history.

Dorothy Bolton, for ever guiltily and romantically conscious of the fact that she was one of those who *had*, waited impatiently, hugging her leather case with her initials stamped in gold on its lid close to her, glancing down the path and wondering what on earth was keeping Stanley.

At seventeen and a half, in the sixth form of the local High School for Girls, she filled out her white blouse with high, well-rounded breasts. Breasts that, restrained only by a liberty-bodice, bobbed embarrassingly up and down as she walked with the rest of her form into assembly, causing some of the younger girls to nudge each other and giggle. Her blue and green striped tie was pinned down to the blouse with her prefect's enamelled badge, and her hat, a much pummelled into shape version of a district nurse's cap, was tucked away out of sight inside the leather case.

If she closed her eyes, she told herself, and counted to a hundred, Stanley would be coming towards her when she opened them. He would come along the path from the nearby Grammar School for Boys, his shabby satchel underneath his arm in the only acceptable way of carrying it, his blue prefect's cap protruding from it, ready to be thrust hastily on his head should he meet a fellow pupil. He would smile at her and sit down beside her, laying one arm across the back of the bench, resting his hand on her shoulder. Ready, if anyone walked past, to lift the hand and pretend to be scratching his head, so as not to compromise her in any way.

'I shall probably join the B.U.F. when I go up to Oxford

at the end of the summer,' he had told her grandly the day before. 'I've given it a lot of thought, and I can't bring myself to believe that the only way of being radical is to be a Commie. In spite of what Stephen Spender says, Russia's social set-up doesn't appeal to me over-much, though they do seem to be escaping the worst of these depressive years.'

Dorothy sighed, opened her eyes, sighed once more, and closed them again. She knew that she was far from stupid, but she was often completely out of her depth when Stanley talked in that way. Politics were rarely mentioned in the red-brick house called Appleroyd in which she lived, except when her father blamed the bloody Government for his shares going down, or her mother wrinkled her nose at the very mention of the word Socialism.

Dorothy did have a dream, however, where she was a woman undergraduate up at Oxford, with a little study all her own. Where she would smoke cigarettes in a long holder, and have brilliant conversations with friends sitting on cushions, putting the world to rights, and listening to Benny Goodman's records. . . .

'I'm sorry I'm late, Dorothy.'

And Stanley was there, standing in front of her, breathing quickly as if he'd run all the way, and wearing, not his school blazer with Cardinal Wolsey emblazoned on its top pocket, but a tweed jacket and dark-grey flannels which fell in folds over the tops of his shoes. His thin face drooped naturally into lines of perpetual anxiety, but as he stood before her on the asphalt path, Dorothy thought his face held the stunned look of the suddenly bereaved.

'You haven't been to school, have you? What's wrong? Have you been ill?' she asked all in one breath.

He came and sat down beside her, looked round furtively, then kissed her cheek before taking a stub of a half-smoked cigarette from the top pocket of his jacket.

'Any objection?' he asked, as he always did.

Dorothy shook her head, feeling tender towards him because of his gentlemanly concern, then waited patiently until he'd used four matches and disappeared behind the turned-up collar of his jacket before getting the cigarette to light.

Then at last, as the tip glowed brightly, he said: 'I can only stop for a minute. I've got to get back home. Something awful has happened, something I can't believe myself.' He turned dark anguished eyes towards her. 'My sister's missing. Our Ruby. We've had the police round to our house, asking questions and everything. My mum's going frantic.'

He dragged heavily at the cigarette stub, holding it as if it were speared on to the end of a pin; glanced at it as if wondering what it might be, then flicked it over the spiked iron railings bordering the duck pond in front of the bench.

Immediately three brown ducks appeared from behind a sheltering bush, and fell on it with angry, frustrated beaks, and Dorothy put her hand on his sleeve in a comforting gesture.

'You mean she's left home? Run off, or something?'

Stanley shook her hand away as if impatient at her lack of understanding. 'No, not run off. *Missing*. You know, like you read in the paper. Missing from home. Disappeared.'

Again the anguish in his eyes dismayed her, and she saw with alarm that he looked as if he'd been crying, as if he might burst into tears there and then. He took her hand and patted it gently between his own. 'She came home as usual from the mill last night, then she had her tea and got ready to go out. With a friend, she said, but I've been telling you for ages how mad she's got lately when Mum's tried to ask her where she goes. "I'm sixteen," she'd say, "and I don't have to account for my every movement. I'm not a kid at school. I bring good money home." You know how she is. I've told you.'

Dorothy put her leather case down beside the bench, suddenly feeling its weight on her knees.

'Yes, I know you told me, and we agreed that she was bound to feel resentful working in the mill while you were still at school, especially with you being two years older than her. Maybe she felt it more than you thought, and she's just gone off to show how unfair she thinks it is.'

Dorothy warmed to her explanation. 'Or perhaps she's had a row with the boy next door she used to go out with. Perhaps she's been secretly fretting for him ever since they finished?'

Stanley's face took on a 'you haven't been listening to me' look, and Dorothy said she was sorry but that she'd only been trying to help.

His mouth actually quivered. 'She took *nothing*. Not her warm coat, not anything. And besides, she's never been that mad at me or at Eddie Marsden from next door. The police asked Mum to search her room to see what was missing, and it's all there, even her Post Office book with three pounds in it. She was saving up for the holiday week at the end of July.' He felt in his pocket for the cigarette stub, and seemed genuinely surprised to find that it was no longer there. 'They're saying that foul play can't be ruled out. You know how they talk . . . I spent most of last night looking for her, going round to her mates' houses and everything, then this morning, before it came light, I went down to the station.'

Dorothy felt his worry transfer itself to her, as if a sudden damp weight was holding her still. Silly phrases such as 'oh well, I expect she'll turn up' or 'she's probably trying to give you and your mother a fright' trembled on her lips, but she didn't say them. How could she, with Stanley sitting beside her on the bench, frozen into anxious silence, pulling at a thread on the sleeve of his jacket, his whole attitude one of such hopelessness that she wanted to put her arms round him and stroke the fear from his thin suffering face?

Sometimes his long dark face reminded her of pictures of Jesus on the Cross, but she had shied away from the thought, feeling it was more than faintly blasphemous.

'Was Ruby worried about anything? Did she *seem* worried

11

at all?' she asked at last, and he muttered that was what the police kept harping on.

'Mum told them that she has three looms in your father's mill, and that she seems to be popular with the other weavers – that everybody likes her.'

'She's very pretty,' he went on, seeing, in his mind's eye, a picture of his young sister, a girl with his own colouring, a gentle girl with black curly hair falling in wispy tendrils over her forehead, soft-eyed, like a misty portrait of a country maid.

'Some of the questions that chap asked,' he said, beating one fist into the other. 'Like was she fond of the lads? Over-fond they meant. Making out that she was a bit of a wrong 'un.' He swallowed hard so that the Adam's apple in his throat moved up and down. 'Mum told him straight that the only boy she's ever been out with is Eddie Marsden next door, and when they checked with him down at the Co-op where he works they found that he'd been in the house all last night.'

Dorothy at last began to see the seriousness of it all. 'How awful!' she said, shaking her head from side to side. 'Is there anything I can do? I have a shorthand and typing lesson in an hour's time, but I can go home now and tell my mother I'm going down to your house . . .'

'Oh, she'd like that all right,' Stanley said with bitterness. 'No, there's nothing anyone can do really, and I'd best be getting back.' He got to his feet, pushing himself up from the bench like an old man with an arthritic hip. 'I won't be going back to school till this lot's sorted out, but I'll try and come here again tomorrow.' He rubbed at his forehead with a clenched fist, then without saying goodbye, started to walk away from her, his head bent as usual, his elbows tucked close into his sides like a long-distance runner.

Dorothy watched him go, then picked up her case. She had a suspicion that his mother cut his hair, as the back always had a kind of torn and ragged look about it. She often thought poetically that it gave him an added vulnerability. Then she started off in the opposite direction, walking as quickly as she could without drawing attention to herself by actually running, because she was late. . . .

'Your Dorothy's late home from school,' Ethel Rostron remarked in a conversational tone to her sister, Phyllis Bolton. Then she rubbed a satisfactory pinch of salt in the wound. 'Is she still friendly with that boy called Stanley Armstrong, out of Inkerman Street?'

'She has netball practice,' Phyllis said quickly, family loyalty decreeing that she didn't let the side down, even if she did happen to be worried out of her mind. Why her younger daughter had to be so different from her sister Margaret, she couldn't think. But then they'd always been like chalk and cheese, the one conforming, and the other always thinking the opposite of what her mother felt she should be thinking.

She patted her hair, but only gingerly as it had been set that morning at the new salon in King Edward Street. An urge to confide her worries to her sister struggled with the desire to keep up her end at all costs. Though it was all very well, she thought privately, for Ethel to be smug, just because her daughter Beryl hadn't even looked at a boy as yet.

'Chance is a fine thing,' she pondered nastily, mentally comparing her own two daughters' fair-haired prettiness with Beryl's own sallow, straight-haired plainness.

'I believe his sister has three looms in Matthew's mill?'

Ethel was all set to get her own back, her jealousy over Margaret's recent engagement to the highly eligible Gerald Tomlin getting the better of her. Gerald, who had come up from London to work as an accountant in Matthew Bolton's mill, was staying with her until the wedding, and his suave manners, plus his undisputed charm, made her sick to her very stomach with envy at times. Beryl was to be brides-maid along with her cousin Dorothy at the wedding in

13

June, and even a mother's love couldn't gloss over the fact that the pale-green taffeta chosen for the dresses would enhance Dorothy's pink and white complexion, whilst making Beryl look as if she were just getting over one of her frequent bilious attacks.

'I've heard tell his mother, Mrs Armstrong I mean, takes in washing, and has done ever since her husband died two years ago. Poor soul,' Ethel added with insincerity.

She was eating afternoon tea at her sister's house, Appleroyd, the biggest of the big red-brick houses overlooking the Corporation Park. Eating with her coat off whilst keeping her hat on.

Keeping one's hat on in the afternoon went with wearing white gloves in Summer, with a spare pair in one's handbag, and with pulling the lavatory chain before one actually sat down so that no one within earshot would know what one was doing. Although Ethel could be earthy and explicit in her language when she chose, she was a great one for inserting ones and whoms into her speech, and usually managed to get them in the right place. The hat toned with her grey tweed dress, and had ear-flaps to show it had been modelled on Amy Johnson's flying helmet.

'They say the poor woman had three "misses" before she managed this boy and his sister,' she said, adjusting the hat with one hand, and reaching for a scone with the other. 'Why their sort always goes in for big families beats me. Goodness knows, French letters are cheap enough.' She pretended not to see Phyllis's expression of disgust. 'Goodness knows, me and Raymond managed without much trouble, though after what I went through with bringing our Beryl into the world I do admit he's always been extra careful, if you know what I mean?' Phyllis obviously did but wasn't prepared to acknowledge it, so she went on, lowering her voice to avoid being overheard by her sister's daily help, a Mrs Wilkinson, working in the kitchen across the hallway. 'Are the Armstrongs *Catholics*?'

'The boy would be at St. Teresa's College if they were,'

Phyllis said, trying not to look as irritated as she felt. 'He's at the Grammar School, and they're Chapel, or so I believe.'

'Well, as long as they're *something* that's the main thing,' Ethel said, 'and I've known some quite nice Methodists,' she went on. She bit into the scone, and a shower of crumbs lodged on her massive shelf of a bosom, made bolster-shaped by the insertion of strategically placed darts in her bust bodice.

They stared at each other for a while with sisterly appraisal, their mouths munching rhythmically.

'Your Mrs Wilkinson has a light hand with scones,' Ethel said, reaching for her third. 'You've been lucky to hang on to her all these years, Phyl. My Mrs Greenhalgh has no more idea of how to bottom a room than fly. It takes her a full half hour to clean my front bay. More interested in what's going on in the road than in what she's doing. You'd think with all this unemployment about she'd want to impress, knowing how many women there are queueing up to earn a few extra shillings a week.'

Phyllis nodded. 'Yes, I know. But they take it from their dole money, Ethel, since this Means Test came in, so it hardly makes it worth their while working.' She lowered her voice to a whisper. 'Mrs Wilkinson is lucky because her husband has a steady job, even though he is on short time at the moment.'

'Hard times,' Ethel said sadly, standing up and showering crumbs on to the carpet. 'Well, I'd best be off. Our Beryl has a piano lesson at five, and I like to be there. He seems a nice enough young man, but you never know. It's the quiet ones one has to keep one's eye on.'

'That's true.'

Phyllis tried not to smile as she agreed through a fleeting vision of her niece Beryl, sitting on the piano stool in the hideously furnished lounge of Tall Trees, her sister's house. Beryl, her ample bottom overflowing the stool, her podgy hands moving laboriously up and down the piano keys, her lank brown hair escaping from its tortoise-shell slide and falling round her plump cheeks. All this whilst her music teacher, the young assistant organist from St. Hilda's Church, struggled with his rising passion.

'No, you can't be too careful,' she said, going with her sister into the hall, and handing her a grey flecked tweed coat from the tall cupboard with hand-carving down its panels.

'Who would be a mother?' Ethel asked as she walked down the drive with her feet at a quarter to three.

'Who indeed?' said Phyllis, closing the vestibule door with a bang so that its red glass panels shivered in protest. A couple of hours of Ethel was quite long enough these days. She'd have to talk to Dorothy about the boy from down Inkerman Street. Perhaps suggest a little musical evening with records on the gramophone, or a light supper with that nice young crowd from the tennis club. She might even get her to invite the Armstrong boy so that she could see him set against boys of her own class. She picked up the tea-tray and carried it through into the kitchen.

Mrs Wilkinson, small, and so thin that her body moved skeleton-like beneath the cross-over pinafore she wore, was taking a satisfied peep at the hot-pot simmering slowly on the middle shelf of the gas oven. Her hair, which should have been grey, was a strange prune colour, due to the cold tea which she combed through it every day, and her bird-bright eyes glittered behind the whirlpool lenses of her spectacles.

'Coming on nicely, Mrs Bolton,' she said. 'I've turned it down as low as it will go; it's the only way to cook hot-pot. Long and low. Same with rice pudding. Sure you wouldn't like me to put one in? Seems a waste of a shelf.'

'Cheese and fruit,' Phyllis said firmly. 'Mr Tomlin's coming tonight, then he's taking Margaret to the cinema. We mustn't make it too heavy a meal.'

She used to say pictures before he came up here, and before she started trying to talk London-posh like he does, Mrs Wilkinson thought, then aloud she said: 'I bet Mr

16

Tomlin's never tasted hot-pot like this in all his natural. They don't know how to cook, Londoners don't. Cucumber sandwiches is all they know about, and he looks as if he could do with a lining on his stomach. If you don't mind me saying so, Mrs Bolton.'

Phyllis wrinkled her nose appreciatively, the conversation with her sister having made her temporarily mindful of her help's undoubted qualities. She leaned forward, a string of amber beads swinging outwards from her chest, noticing the way the potatoes were already taking on the required brown crispness whilst, beneath them, the neck-end chops and the mushrooms cooked themselves into a succulent simmering mash of goodness.

'Mr Tomlin will leave his usual compliments for the chef,' she said with a smile, 'the way he always does when he eats here.'

Mrs Wilkinson beamed, showing a flash of sparkling white false teeth, and a glimpse of artificial gum the shade of a ripe orange.

'That Mrs Greenhalgh, who works for your sister, thinks she's it. Just because her husband's a butter-slapper at the Maypole. And that's all he is, even though he does try to make out that he's the manager. What he brings home in that case he carries is nobody's business, but live and let live, that's what I always say, and always have said.'

She was astute enough to know that Mrs Bolton was shoving up with her, but why should she bother? As long as her pound a week was forthcoming every Friday afternoon, there was no need for her to go moithering herself. It was a nice enough job, with no scrubbing apart from the lino in the kitchen and bathroom, and no windows to clean on account of Philips, the handyman and chauffeur, seeing to them.

And there were plenty of perks. It wasn't for nothing she carried her cross-over pinafore and fur-trimmed bedroom slippers up the hill to Appleroyd every morning bar Sundays in an empty basket. Twelve years she'd worked for

Mrs Bolton now, and hardly a day when she didn't walk back down the hill with a little something in the basket. It might be merely one of Mr Bolton's shirts with slight fray to the cuffs, or it might be a bag of windfalls from the back garden, or even one of her ladyship's cast-off nighties. She always referred to Mrs Bolton as 'her ladyship' when she talked about her to her husband Ned, a porter on the railway.

'What's 'er ladyship come up with today?' he'd ask, having a look in the basket for himself. 'No wonder the country's in the mess it's in when some folks can afford to give good stuff like this away. Better watch yourself if you put that nightie on tonight, lass. See you in that, and I won't be responsible.'

Then he'd twiddle his non-existent moustache and slap his wife on her non-existent behind. A proper caution Ned was, as she was always telling Mrs Bolton.

They had a comfortable relationship as long as she was careful not to overdo the familiarity. Mrs Bolton liked to hear a bit of gossip, in spite of her prim and proper swanky ways, and Mrs Wilkinson had genuinely felt she was doing her employer a good turn when she'd told her about the way Dorothy walked home from school hand in hand with Stanley Armstrong out of Inkerman Street. You couldn't be too careful with girls, and she should know, with both her daughters having to be married. And what went on in the pavilion overlooking the Garden of Remembrance between the High School girls and the Grammar School boys would make your hair curl, even if it was as straight as a drink of water.

'Not that it's any of my business of course,' she'd said, down on her knees in front of the wide tiled fireplace in the lounge, newspapers spread all around her as she cleaned the fire-irons and the brass ornaments off the mantelpiece.

She'd dipped a piece of an old vest recently worn by Mr Bolton into the Brasso. 'The Armstrongs are a clean-living family from what I hear, and it must have been hard going

18

for her since her husband was taken two years back. He worked at the Gas Works, and some say it were the smell what got on his chest.'

Phyllis had tried hard to look as if she thought this possibility was likely. She wanted to find out as much as she could without actually asking questions, but she did wish Mrs Wilkinson would go easy on the Brasso. 'The more you put on the more you will have to rub off,' she had once said mildly, only to have to suffer two days of injured silence as Mrs Wilkinson sulked around the house, sighing into her mid-morning pot of tea. So, despising herself for her weakness, Phyllis merely averted her eyes.

Mrs Wilkinson had then told how poor Mrs Armstrong was forced to take in washing.

'And how she manages with just a living-room with a tiny back scullery leading off it, I don't rightly know. A friend told me that the poor soul has the rollers on her mangle so tight that she's in constant pain with straining over the wheel. With half her insides hanging out I shouldn't wonder.' She reached over for the three brass monkeys in their hear, speak, and see no evil attitudes. 'Their Stanley takes the washing out for her after he finishes school, so it shows he's not got above himself even though he does go to the Grammar School. He's going to the university, you know.'

'A state scholarship,' Phyllis said in some desperation.

Mrs Wilkinson breathed hard on the trio of monkeys. 'All found I believe through a grant or trust or summat. There's no doubt about him being clever, no doubt at all. I've heard his mother goes on about him as if he might be Prime Minister some day.'

'Socialist, of course,' Phyllis had said bitterly.

Two

When Dorothy came in she called out to her mother, then ran straight upstairs to change out of the despised school uniform and to have a good think about Stanley and the way he had looked when he'd told her about his sister.

She couldn't take it seriously somehow. Girls who went missing from home were headlines in newspapers, not girls one knew, and although she had seen Ruby Armstrong in the distance once or twice down at the mill, her impression had been that the girl possessed Stanley's quiet dignity. Certainly not the type to deliberately frighten her mother out of her wits by staying out all night.

No, there would be some explanation . . . perhaps she'd missed a last tram and been afraid to go home. If Mrs Armstrong's determination to see her son through university was anything to go by, she was a strong-willed woman.

She'd had an interesting conversation with Stanley about their respective mothers only the day before, sitting close together on the secluded bench by the duck pond.

'It's a wicked thing to say, but there are times when I'm ashamed and embarrassed by my mother,' she'd said.

She could still recall Stanley's understanding nod.

'It's a perfectly normal part of your growth development, Dorothy. Don't you see? There's often an element of hate in the relationship between a mother and a daughter. Ruby's going through that phase at the moment with our mum. It's a striving for independence, a growing desire to sever the umbilical chord.'

Dorothy unbuttoned her navy-blue serge skirt and stepped out of it. Surely the word hate was a bit much when used in connection with one's mother? It was just that her mother was so . . . so insular-minded. Her horizons were set no further than her own ornately iron-wrought front gate. She wasn't interested in the least about what was going on in Europe, or at the Disarmament Conference, or in the fact that a man called Hitler, a man who loathed the Jews, had recently become the German chancellor. Phyllis didn't want to talk about it. All she wanted to talk about was Margaret's engagement to Gerald Tomlin from London, and the approaching date of the wedding.

'What we need in this country is a leader with fire in his belly,' Dorothy had told her, quoting Stanley, and Phyllis had said. 'Fire in his *stomach*, dear. Belly isn't a nice word for a young girl to use.'

'Thy belly is like an heap of wheat set about with lilies. Thy two breasts are like two young roses that are twins,' Dorothy had replied, just to be difficult. 'You'll be saying that the Song of Solomon isn't nice next.'

'Parts of it are extremely vulgar,' Phyllis had retorted, unabashed.

One thing was certain, Dorothy told herself as she started to roll down her black woollen stockings, her sister Margaret would never want to sever the umbilical chord. It was as if she had obediently fallen in love with Gerald Tomlin just to please her mother. Because, as a continuation of the good little girl she had always been, she could be happy only if her parents were happy.

Muttering to herself as she rummaged in the untidiness of her dressing-table drawer for a pair of lisle stockings, Dorothy asked herself how any girl of twenty-one, as pretty as Margaret, could be smitten with a man in his middle thirties with sandy hair, freckles, and wet lips? Personally she found him utterly repulsive with his charm laid on with a trowel, and his yellow spotted cravats, not to mention the hideous Max Baer pouched sports jackets he chose to wear.

To love a man like that . . . ugh! It was enough to make one feel sick, she told herself, turning round and checking that the seams of her stockings were straight. Then she wondered vaguely whether to tell her father about the lecture they'd had that day at school about careers in the Civil Service. The prospect of going to work in the mill office appalled her, even though the draughty little building was situated down a long flagged slope, well away from the deafening clatter of the looms in the weaving shed.

Which brought her thoughts back full circle to Ruby Armstrong. No wonder she'd run away. What chance had *she* had to improve her station by learning shorthand and typing privately? What chance of anything with a brother as brilliantly clever as Stanley, and with a mother who washed other people's clothes all day so that her son could stay on at school and pass one exam after another?

Dorothy opened her wardrobe door and took out her favourite dress of the moment, blue crêpe with white spots and a white floppy organdie bow at the neckline.

It was certainly funny that Ruby hadn't taken any of her clothes with her, but then she'd probably had this wild romantic notion of walking out of the house into the arms of her lover – because surely there was a lover somewhere? – with nothing but the clothes she stood up in. It was like a story out of a magazine. Like the beginning of a serial in one of the *Woman Pictorials* Mrs Wilkinson brought to the house.

Leaving everything behind, everything she had held most dear, she walked away to a fresh beginning, a new life with the man who loved her from the depths of his very soul. . . .

'Are you there, Dorothy?' Margaret Bolton put her head round the door then came in and walked straight over to the mirror.

'Just look at my hair,' she said without preamble. 'Gerald's coming to dinner, and I haven't time to wash it and get it dry. It's been one hell of a day at the office. Mr

Martin gave me four letters to type at the last minute, then he made me do one over again. He might be the Education Officer, but he's hopeless at putting words together.' She held out a strand of her fair hair. 'Do you think if I wet the ends with sugared water and put a few curlers in, it would curl up in time?'

'It looks all right to me,' Dorothy said, easing her feet into black court shoes without glancing in her sister's direction. 'Anyway, when you marry your Gerald, he'll have to see you looking a mess sometimes. Will you be sleeping in curlers like you do now, with Ponds cold cream on your face?'

'Of course not. I'll wait until he's gone to the mill, then I'll put my curlers in underneath a turban.'

Margaret was answering quite seriously, having thought this out only the week before. 'Gerald doesn't even like me putting my lipstick on or powdering my nose in front of him. He likes his women to look as if they make no effort at all to look pretty.'

'His *women*?' Dorothy raised an eyebrow.

'A joke,' Margaret, who never made them, said. Then leaning closer to the mirror she pulled at her half-fringe, tram-lines of anxiety furrowing her broad forehead. 'I wish you'd try to be nicer to Gerald, our Dorothy. He's not all that happy at the moment having to stay with Auntie Ethel and Uncle Raymond until the wedding. Uncle Raymond is always talking about what it was like in the trenches in Flanders Fields all those years ago, and Beryl stares at him.'

'Stares at him? Whatever for?'

'Gerald thinks it's because she has a crush on him. She does it when they're having a meal, and he says he can't chew his food properly because every time he looks up from his plate, there she is. Staring at him.'

'Well, at least he can't accuse me of that,' Dorothy said, running a comb through her thick curly hair and being glad it curled naturally and didn't have to be helped along with hot water with sugar melted into it.

'Stanley Armstrong's sister's missing,' she said all at once.

Margaret turned round from the mirror looking so much like her mother that Dorothy flinched.

'You mean that boy out of Inkerman Street? His sister?'

'You know very well who I mean. You must have heard Mother telling me how I'm lowering myself being friendly with a boy like that.'

'There's no need to get so uppity for heaven's sake.'

Dorothy jerked at the narrow belt on her frock. 'She's for ever reminding me how lovely the boys at the tennis club are, and urging me to join the Young Conservatives. And why I have to learn shorthand and typing privately when I could leave school in July and go to the Technical College in September, I don't know. Is there some virtue in paying for education? I have to mingle with the scholarship girls at school after all.'

'You've got Bolshie ideas, our Dorothy. And I knew something was wrong when I telephoned Gerald at the mill. He sounded quite upset and he said the police were there. Something to do with one of the girl weavers, he said.'

Dorothy tweaked the organdie bow into position, and leaning round her sister at the dressing-table, outlined her lips with purple lipstick then wiped it off again.

So Stanley had been right. They were treating it as foul play. Mrs Armstrong must have convinced the police that her daughter would never have stayed out all night without letting her know. She felt the gloom of unease settle around her as if someone had suddenly draped a damp blanket over her shoulders. She wanted for some inexplicable reason to take her feelings out on Margaret who was watching her now with a martyred expression on her face. The shorthand lesson loomed ahead in her mind like the promise of some medieval torture, and she wanted her sister to retaliate to her mood by shouting at her, or at least by walking out of

24

the room and slamming the door. There were times when she could hear herself being nasty, and the feeling was strangely exhilarating.

'A demonstration of one's baser feelings is common,' her mother had told her once. 'Anyone would think you were a mill girl at times, Dorothy. In clogs and shawl.'

Dorothy hadn't bothered to remind her mother that the girls at her father's mill never wore clogs and shawls; that it was Grandma Lipton, Phyllis's mother, who had gone to work dressed like that, being knocked up by a man called Daft Jack who walked the early morning streets, rattling on the windows of the terraced houses with a stick with umbrella spokes on the end of it. To mention this would have tightened Phyllis's mouth into a grim line, and frozen her neat features into a mask of distaste.

It was for this reason that Grandma Lipton had never been brought from the Nursing Home to be there when Gerald Tomlin was visiting.

'She does it on purpose,' Phyllis had said. 'She's proud of the way we've got on in one way, and yet in another she resents it.'

'Look, Dorothy,' Margaret was saying, her interest in the missing Armstrong girl having evaporated, 'I wish you'd just try and be nicer to Gerald. He'll be Father's partner in the mill one day; he's taken the financial side over altogether now, and when we're married he'll be your brother-in-law, remember. We'll be living not all that far away, and you'll be coming to see us often I hope.' She opened her blue eyes wide in accusation. 'He knows you don't like him, you know.'

'He probably thinks it's because I've fallen for him and am madly jealous that you're the one he's chosen, him being God's gift to women,' Dorothy said, biting her lip and turning away.

She knew she could never tell Margaret the main reason for her active dislike of the elegant young man from London. Just how, for heaven's sake, did you tell someone with their wedding coming up in June that you wouldn't trust their precious fiancé any further than you could throw him?

Her real aversion to Gerald Tomlin had started the day she had seen him flirting with one of the mill girls as they streamed out of the yard on their way home late one afternoon. He was leaning against his red MG sports car, a fawn raincoat tightly belted round his waist, a cigarette held casually in his long fingers, and what he was saying was making the young girl giggle in a familiar way that would have made Phyllis's blood run cold. She was a big girl, with the front piece of her hair peroxided to a white candy-floss, and as Dorothy watched unseen from the office window, Gerald had suddenly turned her round and fondled her plump behind before giving it a resounding slap.

She wasn't a prude, heavens, not that, and she wasn't a snob, heavens not that either, but it wasn't quite in keeping with the gentlemanly behaviour he displayed when he came to Appleroyd. Perhaps there was more of her mother in her than she realized. . . .

No, she could never tell Margaret, nor could she tell her that the New Year's kiss she had received from Gerald had disgusted her and almost made her feel sick.

It was what the girls at school would have described as a French kiss, with his slack mouth opening over her own, and his tongue probing wetly and rhythmically.

It had been almost a case of incest, she had told herself dramatically afterwards, and had wondered how Margaret, her fastidious, prim, and reserved sister could possibly put up with it? Compared with that nauseating kiss, Stanley's kisses were hard and fierce. And very much to be preferred, she decided.

'Are you very much in love with Gerald?' she asked, trying to imagine Margaret responding to such a sickly embrace. And failing.

'What a thing to ask!'

Margaret fiddled with the silver-backed brush on the

26

dressing-table, the back of her neck going slightly pink. 'You've been reading Mrs Wilkinson's *Woman Pictorials* again, haven't you?' She gazed up at the ceiling as if searching for the right words. 'Life isn't a bit like it's set up to be in those stories you know.'

'No, you're right. Life is like Gerald Tomlin,' Dorothy said, not quite underneath her breath. Then feeling ashamed of herself, left the room and went downstairs to set the seal on her nasty mood by lying to her mother about the mythical netball practice. Getting so carried away that she even described the way she had hurled the ball into the net from a distance of at least ten yards. . . .

She was back from the typing lesson just in time to sit down at the dinner table with the family. She had been driven back by Philips, and he'd told her there had been a police car in the mill yard all the afternoon.

'Right excitement there were in the weaving sheds,' he'd said with some satisfaction. 'Tongues clacking almost as loud as the looms. They say they're thinking of dragging the duck pond in the Corporation Park.'

'Why?'

'Because that's where all the courting couples go, isn't it?'

She blushed and hoped Philips hadn't noticed, but he had changed the subject, and anyway he wasn't interested in what she did, only at the moment in telling her about his lady friend's mother, who apparently was on her deathbed, which meant he could marry Vera at last.

He was a neat man, with tiny hands and a bald head which he concealed beneath his peaked cap. What bit of hair he had was plastered to his scalp with solidified brilliantine, and he had a habit of smacking his lips at the end of each sentence, which must, Dorothy had often thought, drive his fiancée mad.

'The problem is that Vera wants us to live in her house in

27

Charlotte Street, but I don't want to give my little place up,' he said, with a loud expressive smack of the lips. 'I've just got it to my liking with a back-boiler in the living-room that heats the water a treat. But Vera's adamant.'

He pronounced it as 'adayment', and Dorothy, over the blush now, thought of Vera, who could have been any age between forty and sixty, and who wore her black hair in pin-wheel plaits over each ear, and sported white ankle socks over her stockings. Vera ran the Church Guide Troop at St. Hilda's as if the patrols were training for military manoeuvres, and the very idea of her lying by Philip's side in a double bed filled Dorothy with a kind of hysterical horror. Gerald Tomlin had said that Philips was a pansy and would never marry, and that Vera was a natural spinster, clinging to her invalid mother and making her an excuse not to marry.

'They're born virgins, the two of them,' he had said, making sure that Mrs Bolton was well out of earshot before using a word that she would have considered indelicate. 'Any couple who court for over twenty years have no intention of marrying. I've seen the inside of Philips's house, and no woman could keep it as clean and tidy as that.'

Dorothy had felt bound to agree, having seen with her own eyes a potted plant on a doyley on the draining board in the kitchen, and covers covering the covers on the three-piece suite in the front parlour.

'I bet he goes to bed with his vest on underneath his pyjama jacket,' Gerald went on, and Dorothy's father, who did exactly that, had merely grunted as he'd come into the room and caught the tail-end of the conversation.

Matthew Bolton's big face settled into lines of content-ment as his younger daughter took her place at the dinner table.

'Hallo, chuck,' he said, winking at her, and thinking what a corker she looked in that blue spotted dress. By the heck but she were a bonny lass, even though from the expression on her face she looked as if she might be spoiling for a fight as usual. Always asking questions there weren't no answers to, and not knowing what it was she wanted to do when she left school. Wondering what life was all about, and worriting about things far beyond her control, things she could do nowt about. Not like Margaret there, who took it all for granted. He beamed again at Dorothy who wrinkled her nose at him affectionately.

He'd been doing a bit of wondering about life himself lately, come to that. What with the worry of them bloody Japs modernizing more and more of their cotton mills, and supplying the British markets at a price he couldn't hope to compete with. Not with the overheads he'd got. Already he'd scrapped a third of his looms, and a good job it was he'd stuck to his father's maxim of not spending a penny unless he could put his hand in his back pocket and cover it with another. And still seeing his family went short of nowt into the bargain.

At the other end of the long mahogany table, his wife was presiding over the brown dish of hot-pot, as regally as if it were a gold-plated dish, her hands daintily occupied as she passed the plates round.

'Typed any good letters, Dorothy?'

Gerald Tomlin was smiling at her with his freckled pouchy face, his wet eyes glistening with anticipation as he took a plate of food from his prospective mother-in-law.

Everything about him is wet, Dorothy thought, with the familiar feeling of distaste. His hair shines too much, and his lips look as if he'd just licked them ready to give one of his awful sloppy kisses.

'I'll never be as good a secretary as Margaret,' she told him, being polite and rather humble for her sister's sake. 'This evening we had to type in time to a military two-step on the gramophone, and the keys on my typewriter kept on coming up all jammed together. I think I'd have been better off with a funeral dirge.'

Gerald threw back his sandy head and laughed as if she'd said something unbearably witty. He laughed so much that there was almost a touch of hysteria in it, and he really was pathetic, Dorothy thought with distaste. Then saw the expression on her sister's face, and seeing, got the answer to the question she had asked earlier.

Margaret was in love. Really in love. The head-over-heels kind so strongly advocated in Mrs Wilkinson's magazines. She must have been at her hair with the sugar and water, Dorothy decided, for now it curved softly on to her flushed cheeks; her eyes shone blue, and when she smiled her mouth was a soft and dreamy curve of content-ment. She studied her sister's face with a morbid fascination. Margaret seemed to be smiling affectionately at the hot-pot on her plate, pushing it gently from side to side, almost as if she found its beauty too much to bear.

'The time I start smiling at hot-pot I'll know I'm really sunk,' Dorothy told herself, and made up her mind to go on trying to be nice to Gerald.

'I like your tie,' she told him, knowing this remark was sure to please as Gerald was a snazzy dresser. And at once he beamed round the table and told them all that it was hand-made silk from Harrods in London, and that with the matching crêpe silk handkerchief peeping from his top pocket, it had set him back all of twelve and sixpence.

'But worth every penny, Gerald,' Phyllis said, and Dorothy tried not to raise her eyebrows as she remembered the times her mother had reminded her that to mention the cost of anything was extremely common.

'I even put Mrs Wilkinson's wages in an envelope so that I don't have the embarrassment of handing her the actual money,' she'd once said.

It was no good, Dorothy told herself, she couldn't bring herself to like the bland young man sitting by her sister's side. She would try, just as she was trying now not to mention the intruding worry in her mind of Ruby Armstrong's disappearance. She knew how much her mother hated controversial and serious subjects being aired at the table. And Phyllis had gone to a lot of trouble, ladling the hot-pot into her best Wedgwood dinner plates, and using the silver knives and forks from the polished mahogany case on the sideboard.

'Unpleasant subjects should always be kept from the table,' was another of her sayings, and Dorothy knew she wouldn't be able to bear it if the missing girl was mentioned and her mother said, as she was bound to say, that she had got what she was probably asking for.

'If she said that I would just walk out,' Dorothy told herself silently, and watched Gerald being pressed, obviously against his will, to accept a second helping.

'My compliments to the chef,' he said, just as she had known he would say.

It was no good. She couldn't keep silent after all. She had to ask. She could still see Stanley's thin face, noble with suffering, and the police might have told her father something? Perhaps even now Ruby was weeping on her mother's shoulder, saying that she didn't know what had made her do such a dreadful thing; swearing that she didn't mind working at the mill, that she fully understood that anyone as brilliant as her brother had to have his chance.

'I heard today . . .' she began.

'Margaret and I . . .' Gerald said at the same time.

'Sorry,' Dorothy said. And the moment was gone.

Gerald smiled, showing white teeth as small as a child's first milk teeth. 'I'm taking Margaret to the Rialto, to the Second House. Would you like to come with us, Dorothy? I could sit between you; a thorn between two roses, what?'

Dorothy thanked him, and explained quite truthfully that she had piles of homework to do. Then, as Gerald started talking about the film, she decided that being nice wasn't a virtue at all. It was merely the way one wanted to be at a given time. A form of self indulgence, in fact.

What hypocrites we are, she thought, every one of us.

'I saw the film in London at the beginning of the year,' Gerald was saying. 'Charles Laughton makes a topping Henry the Eighth, and Merle Oberon as Anne Boleyn is

31

simply superb.' He waved his fork about to add emphasis to his words. 'She is that marvellous and rare thing, a stunning woman with intelligence as well as beauty.' He patted Margaret's face to show he meant no offence. 'And Robert Donat . . . well . . .' Words seemed to fail him. 'He takes the part of Catherine Howard's lover, and his voice is superb, sort of hoarse with a marvellous sense of feeling in it, if you know what I mean. Superb,' he said again.

Dorothy leaned forward, forgetting it was Gerald she was talking to, and not Stanley.

'I read that they show the jovial side of the King's nature, not his selfish cruelty. Surely that's all wrong?'

Gerald smiled his shiny smile. 'People go to the cinema to be entertained, not to witness the unsavoury details of history, my dear.'

Dorothy gave up trying to be agreeable. 'That's just silly. If the film people want to show actual characters who lived and breathed, then they should show them as they were, warts and all. So why can't we be shown Henry as he was, with all his unsavoury habits, and his . . .'

Gerald's smile dimmed a little. 'Perhaps until you see the film for yourself . . . ?'

Ignoring the warning glances her mother was sending her from across the table, Dorothy said that she was in all probability going to see it with a friend on Saturday.

'Which friend?' her mother asked, forcing her to lie, and realizing from the knowing look on Gerald's face that he knew that she was lying.

Oh God, she thought miserably, why did her family hang on to his every word as if he were Moses? Couldn't they see that he would break Margaret's heart? Why, oh why, couldn't her sweet and kind sister have fallen in love with Edwin Birtwistle, the captain of the tennis club for three consecutive seasons, a director in his father's firm at twenty-five? Edwin Birtwistle would have loved Margaret for ever more, and never ever kissed her sister with his mouth wide open, or fondled another girl's bottom in broad daylight.

'I had been thinking that perhaps you and I could go to the First House tomorrow night, dear,' her mother was saying, her beads making little clattering noises on the edge of the table as she stacked the plates together. 'Your father has a Rotary meeting, and we could have high tea in the Emporium Café first.'

'I am going with a friend on Saturday,' Dorothy said in some despair, wishing she could say the friend was Stanley. Wishing he could come to the house like Gerald Tomlin, and be accepted and listened to. Wishing they could hear the marvellous way he talked, his dark eyes eager, his voice going gruff when he talked about a subject dear to his heart.

Wishing he wasn't going away. . . .

Three

After Stanley had left Dorothy in the park, he ran all the way down West Road with a long loping stride, his elbows tucked into his sides and his grasshopper legs covering the ground at an incredible rate, like a long-distance runner.

The houses, set well back from the road, were ivy-covered, solid and secluded in their respectability, a different world away from the mean street in which he lived. A group of girls in scarlet blazers and peaked caps were coming out of the private school on the corner, and a girl with a bold face called something out to him, but hearing nothing, he ran on.

At the bottom of the road, on the main trunk thorough-fare were the tram-lines, running parallel all the way into the town. For a moment he hesitated as he heard the rattle and whine of an approaching tram, calculating whether it would be quicker to catch it or take a short cut back to the house.

Already his breath was catching in his throat, and there was a stabbing, pricking pain in his left side, but he didn't slacken his pace, running along for a while at the side of the tram, then turning into a street of Victorian houses which had been turned into solicitors' offices.

He'd had no right to leave his mother alone, he knew that now, but it had seemed important that Dorothy shouldn't be kept waiting; that he told her what had happened before she heard it from her father. And his mother had under-stood. Or at least she had seemed to understand.

'It's the waiting,' she'd kept saying all the long day, 'The waiting, and feeling so helpless like.'

He had left her ironing a pile of shirts heaped high in her ironing basket. Standing at the living-room table with the familiar folded blanket in place. Slipping the heated flat-iron into its polished slipper while the second iron hotted up at the blazing coal fire.

'How can you work at a time like this?' he'd asked her, and she'd gone on working without looking up.

'If I stopped doing something I'd go out of my mind. It's the waiting, you see,' she'd said again.

On he ran, along a wide street lined with shops, a third of them closed and shuttered, with slogans written on their empty windows. UP THE BOLSHIES. DOWN WITH THE MEANS TEST. Past a massive poster proclaiming that EVERYWHERE YOU CAN BE SURE OF SHELL. Past a tripe shop with the white honeycombed offal laid out in the window on a marble slab, flanked by pigs' trotters, and a pig's head with an orange in its mouth.

Past a chip shop, almost knocking over a woman coming out with a basin of fish and chips covered with a white cloth . . . reminding him that he was hungry.

Into the labyrinth now of steep streets with terraced houses opening straight on to the pavements, with house-wives standing on their doorsteps, gossiping, arms folded over the flowered cross-over pinafores they wore like a uniform, keeping watchful eyes on their children as they played hopscotch, using the flagged pavements as their marking grounds.

On through a back passage, slipping on the greasy cobblestones, ducking under lines of washing, past a small boy walking with legs wide apart, sobbing loudly because he'd wet himself. Seeing it all. And seeing nothing.

And as he turned into Inkerman Street, they were there, the vultures, pretending to be stoning their window-bottoms, some of them mopping their front steps and the surrounding flags for the third time that day. Turning eager

35

eyes towards him as he ran panting to number twenty-seven.

'Is there any news, love?'

That was Mrs Crawley from across the street, a neighbour who spent all day wearing her husband's flat cap and an apron made out of sacking, and went out each night wearing a tight black suit and a pillar-box hat with an eye veil. Rouged to kill and up to no good, as everyone said. She *would* be the only one with the nerve to ask outright, Stanley thought, and shook his head. Not because he wished to snub her, but because there wasn't the breath left to speak.

And besides, Mrs Crawley had the right to ask if anyone had. The street's official benefactor, she was the first one called on when a laying-out became necessary. Propped against her back-yard wall was a spare lavatory door, kept for such a purpose.

'Keeps 'em nice and straight,' she would say, laying the corpse out flat on its unyielding surface, closing the eyes for the last time with pennies weighting down the lids, arranging the lifeless hands in a neatly folded praying position over the newly washed chests. No point in paying the undertaker when Mrs Crawley would do it for no more than a cup of tea or a glass of throat-stinging ginger wine.

Mrs Crawley it was who had scrubbed the oilcloth in Ruby's room till the pattern had almost vanished when Ruby had been taken off in the ambulance to the fever hospital burning with diphtheria two years before. Making the entire house reek to the rooftops of Jeyes Fluid for days to come.

Mrs Crawley who had sat up with the three-year-old Ruby when the pneumonia had almost finished her. Sitting up all night so that her mother could get some rest. Keeping the steam kettle going, changing the sheets from under her when the fever broke and she lay bathed in sweat. Searching the town on a Sunday afternoon when Ruby, over the crisis, fancied a bit of ice-cream.

Oh, yes. Mrs Crawley had the right to ask. . . .

'Mum! I'm back!' Stanley called out as he closed the front door behind him. 'I wasn't long, was I? I told you I wouldn't be.'

But the woman who turned her face towards him as he walked down the passage, past the front parlour, and into the living-room, was a woman for whom time had lost all meaning. One hour, or two, or three, what did it matter? All she was waiting for was the knock on the door to say that Ruby had been found safe and well. The other supposition she would not countenance. So she did what she had to do, as if she'd been wound up inside, all her being concentrating on the shirt she was ironing on the table in front of her.

Otherwise she'd crack, and she knew it.

Double bits first. Cuffs, neck-band, button-trim, wrong side first. Spitting on the iron first to see if it was the right heat. She could tell that by the way the spit bounced off and slid along the gleaming slipper. Stiff collars, damp dry from the big basin of starch with a dab of dolly-blue in it. Collars ironed to a polished smoothness with the iron running over a piece of fent from the mill. The mill . . . Oh God, that's where her Ruby should be at that moment, standing at her looms on the wet flagged floor with her flowered overall over her dress, and her dark curly hair wisping softly round her bonny face. Back to the collars. Curving them round her hand, then layering them one inside the other, making sure the fold was in the right place.

When she saw Stanley she straightened up for a moment and stared at him through dark eyes sunk deep into their sockets with worry and exhaustion. She laid the iron on its rest for a moment.

'They came again while you were gone. He said they were going to drag the duck pond in the Corporation Park at first light tomorrow. Seems one of her work-mates was standing by the side gate in West Road last night about ten o'clock with a boy, and thought she saw Ruby go in with a boy. Or a man. She couldn't see either of them; didn't look really, but she thought it might have been our Ruby's voice.'

'Oh, Mum. . . .'

Stanley went to her and gently brushed the hair away from her hot forehead. It was unbelievable how in one short day his mother's looks had changed to what he imagined they might be when she was an old, old woman. Surely flesh could not sag in the space of twenty-four hours? Less than that. Deep wrinkles appearing where wrinkles had never been before?

In spite of her long hours at the dolly-tub, fishing clothes out of the boiler with the rounded stick, and her back-breaking stretches at the mangle with its wide wooden rollers, Ada Armstrong was a handsome woman. The country freshness of her Cumberland upbringing had never quite left her cheeks, and her hair, black and coarse as wire, without a single strand of silver in it, sprang away from her forehead, refusing to lie smooth.

Stanley gave her a push towards the rocking chair set by the fire. 'Sit down, Mum. Just for a few minutes. I'll get you a cup of tea.' His mind shied away from what she had just told him. They couldn't think . . . not the duck pond in the park? Not the very place he'd just left with the wind rippling its dark green surface? Ruby with her hair, her pretty hair caught up in the long grasses, her body bloated and swollen . . . 'They don't know anything; it's only that they have to follow up any kind of lead they get. Please sit down, Mum. To please me. You'll be ill.'

So to please him Ada sat down for a second on the very edge of the chair, then got up and followed him through into the scullery.

'She wouldn't be going in the park with a boy at that time, not our Ruby. She was always in by ten. Besides she always told me where she was going, and last night she was going with a mate from work to the Bulb Show in town then back to this girl's house.'

'Which girl, Mum?' Stanley filled the kettle and found a

match for the gas. 'They haven't found her yet, have they?' He had to make her *think* however cruel it might seem to be. His logical mind couldn't accept that there was nothing, not a single clue. In spite of her recent secretiveness, Ruby was an honest girl, with every expression on her face there for all to read. He had to try again.

'Did she ever even hint to you that she had found herself another boy? Even give you the slightest suspicion that she was doing something she had no right to be doing?'

Ada followed him to the cupboard as he reached for two cups and put them side by side on the draining board. Her usually clear voice was low. 'What I've been thinking I don't rightly like to say.'

Stanley went back to the kettle and she followed him there. 'You must say it, Mum. Even if it doesn't seem important. You must say it.'

Ada sighed a deep sigh. 'Ever since she packed it in with Eddie Marsden next door, she's been different. Keeping herself to herself, and snapping at me when I've tried to talk to her.'

The kettle came to the boil and Stanley carried it over to the teapot, his mother no more than a step behind him.

'I think she's been going out with a married man. Oh yes, I do, and you don't need to look like that, son, because them what's never come up against temptation don't know what they're saying.'

Carefully Stanley poured the hot water out in a steady stream. 'There's a Spanish proverb that says "He who avoids the temptation avoids the sin." I wasn't shocked, Mum.'

'It all fits in somehow. She's been telling me lies, that's obvious. The sergeant told me she hasn't been seeing the girls at the mill, not if they were telling the truth, that is. But they couldn't tell him anything. Not a word, so she's been just as secretive with them as she has with me. I know my girl and she was probably too ashamed to tell anyone what was going on, don't you see?'

Without waiting for the tea to brew Stanley poured it into the cups, laced them both liberally with sugar, and went out to the small meat safe in the yard where they kept the milk.

'You mean you think she's gone off with this . . . this married chap?'

'Aye, I do.'

'Without taking her warm coat, or her nightdress, or anything?'

He carried the cups into the living-room and set them down on the table next to the pile of ironing. Then, although the room was hot to the point of suffocation, he lifted a square slab of coal from the scuttle and put it on the fire. At that moment warmth spelt comfort somehow . . . Guiding his mother to the rocking chair he put the cup of tea in her hands.

'Look, Mum, you could be right. I hope you are right, but I can't think, I can't believe . . .' He sat down opposite to her in the big armchair that had been his father's. 'Anyway if you are right, all the police have to do is to check on some poor woman whose husband didn't come home last night. She'd be bound to report him missing to the police, wouldn't she, just as we did our Ruby?'

'Perhaps he doesn't come from this town? Perhaps he's just in digs here?'

'Then his landlady would report it. Mum, that still doesn't explain why she didn't smuggle some of her clothes out of the house. You know what she's like about her things. She creates every time anybody touches anything. No, I can't believe she would leave the lot behind.'

'Are you trying to prepare me for the fact that she's dead?'

Stanley quickly denied this. 'No, of course I'm not. I just feel that by talking round it we may dig up some reason. It's making us *think*, Mum, the way the sergeant asked us to do.'

Ada still hadn't put the cup to her lips. She was staring

40

into the fire now, wrinkling her brow as she tried to concentrate.

'She didn't take anything out with her because it was *unpremeditated*. That's why. She met this chap and they decided to go away on the spur of the moment, and when they think the dust's settled a bit Ruby will write to us. She always did get carried away. Look how she thought she was madly in love with Eddie next door.' Ada turned towards Stanley eagerly, willing him, willing herself to believe she had stumbled on a rational explanation. 'And why did she finish with Eddie? There were never a proper reason for that now, were there?'

'She was . . . is only sixteen,' Stanley corrected himself quickly, horrified at his slip of the tongue. 'She told me herself that she thought the girls at the mill were daft, drifting into marriage with the first boy they went out with. She told me a lot of them are back at their looms now, with their mothers looking after their babies.'

'She wanted better than Eddie,' his mother said as if he had never spoken. 'His mother came in for a minute while you were out, and she says that when Eddie came home for his dinner he told her the police had been to the shop asking him questions. She said the manager was quite upset and insisted on shutting them in the store room at the back to talk.'

Stanley watched her with love, ready to take the cup from her hands.

She was so tired, he realized, she scarcely knew what she was saying. But she was drinking the tea now, taking great gulps of it, and the glow from the fire was bringing back the colour to her cheeks. Perhaps he could persuade her to eat something? A boiled egg? Stanley felt he could manage that without too much difficulty.

'Are there any eggs, Mum?' he was saying when the knock came to the door, a knock followed by Mrs Crawley's voice calling out 'Can I come in, Mrs Armstrong?'

She was already in, a bright yellow headscarf covering

the curlers in her hair, holding a basin covered with a tea cloth out before her. 'Now I don't want no refusals,' she said, putting the basin down on the table next to the basket of unironed shirts. 'And you can call me an interfering old bugger if you've a mind to, but I reckoned you wouldn't be feeling like cooking for your teas, not just now. So I've been down to the chip shop, and there's two two's and a pennorth of dabs each, all salted and vinegared, ready to eat, and I wouldn't bother with plates if I was you. Just get 'em down as they are. Fingers was made before forks, as Shakespeare said.'

To his dismay Stanley saw the way his mother's face crumpled, and the way she looked down at the cup in her hands, biting hard on her lips. That was his mum all over . . . worry she could take, poverty she could cope with, heartbreak too, but kindness – that was another thing altogether. Kindness demoralized her. It seemed as if she was at a loss to know how to deal with it; so over the years she had armoured herself against it. Built a dirty great wall up around herself, making it plain that independence was all, that a kindness could only be accepted on her own terms.

'I'll get me purse,' she said and walked over to the top drawer in the sideboard.

'That'll be eightpence then, Mrs Armstrong,' Mrs Crawley added, knowing her neighbour too well to protest, and holding out her hand for the money. 'By gum, but there's been more steps mopped in this street today than I've seen in all the years I've lived here,' she told Stanley as he walked with her down the lobby to the front door. 'Any more news yet, love?'

He shook his head. 'Thanks for the chips, Mrs Crawley.' He hesitated. 'And thanks for not asking her any questions.' He jerked his head backwards.

Nellie Crawley's usually gruff voice was soft. 'How's she bearing up then, lad?'

'She'll have to get some sleep tonight or she'll crack. I'm

42

wondering if I ought to go down to the chemist's and ask him for something to give her before he closes.'

Nellie gave him a none too gentle punch in the shoulder. 'Don't waste your time, love. She wouldn't take it, and I wouldn't blame her. She'll want to know the minute there's any news, not be sound asleep under the influence of old Brandwood's herbal concoctions.'

'You're right, Mrs Crawley.'

She started to walk away. 'I'm *always* right, love. That's what gets me old man down, the fact that I'm always right. Now you go back in and see she eats them chips while they're hot.'

But when Stanley walked back into the living-room, his mother was weeping silently into the covered basin, holding it in her arms and rocking it backwards and forwards as if it were a child.

A child she had lost and never thought to see again.

Four

After Margaret and Gerald had left for the second-house pictures, holding hands and smiling at each other, Dorothy helped her mother with the dishes.

'Why don't you just stack them and leave them for Mrs Wilkinson to do in the morning?' Dorothy asked, and her mother said it wasn't in her nature to leave the kitchen a mess.

'You can always tell a woman's character by the tidiness or otherwise of her kitchen,' she said, and looking round at the gleaming surfaces and the hanging cups all facing the same way, Dorothy could see that this was true.

Phyllis's character was unblemished by a single idiosyncrasy; her thoughts faced all the same way like the blue and white cups; she spoke in clichés, and even they were polished to grammatical perfection before she uttered them. She seemed to have forgotten what she would have called the argument, and what Dorothy would have called the discussion about the film at the dinner table. She wore an apron with a frill round it, tied in an immaculate bow over her high-necked woollen dress, and she washed the dishes, using both rubber gloves and a little mop at the end of a stick, and talked about the hat she couldn't find for the wedding.

'It's no use. I'll have to decide on navy blue and get gloves and shoes to match. It's the done thing to have all one's accessories to tone,' she said, handing Dorothy a plate, 'in a darker shade than one's outfit. I think I'll get

44

that obliging little Mrs Pearson in the hat market to put a piece of ribbon in the same turquoise as my suit round the brim of my hat. What do you think?' She pushed a strand of hair away from her forehead with a rubber encased hand. 'I can't make up my mind whether it will give my outfit a put-together look, or make it appear a bit on the home-made side.'

Dorothy dragged her thoughts back from Inkerman Street and what might be going on there. 'It's a good job Gerald hasn't got any parents, or you'd be having to consult with his mother to make sure you didn't clash.'

Phyllis held up a fork to the light, considered it done, and slotted it into the big white jug on the draining board. 'The bride's mother always has first choice as to colours,' she said, very seriously. 'Poor Gerald. He's bound to feel it on the day, not having any relatives on his side. I've told him I'm arranging for some of ours to sit in the right hand pews to even things up a bit.'

Escaping with relief, Dorothy found her father upstairs in the big front bedroom exchanging his dark grey office jacket for the woollen cardigan he would have worn if Gerald hadn't been to dinner. Caught off-guard he looked tired almost to the point of exhaustion, with purple sagging pouches underneath his eyes, and a too hectic flush on his cheeks.

Dorothy came straight to the point.

'Dad. I was talking to Stanley Armstrong after school, and he told me that his sister Ruby, one of your weavers, is missing from home. He said the police had been to the mill. What do you make of it?'

Matthew Bolton yanked off his tie and gave her a shrewd glance from beneath his thick wildly curling eyebrows. No use trying to fob off this younger daughter of his with soothing words. Ask her dad a question and she got the answer straight, the way he knew she wanted it.

'Aye, it's a bad business, love. The police seem to be convinced in their minds that it isn't the usual case of a

45

young girl leaving home and catching the train down to London to the bright lights, to show her folks something or other. They're tying it up with those two murders out Barnoldswick way last winter. They never caught whoever did them, and this case has all the hallmarks.' He fought a losing battle with his back collar stud. 'Pretty young girl with a recent history of secretiveness at home, telling lies where she goes of nights. But they can't prove a thing till they find . . .'

'A body,' Dorothy finished for him. 'Oh, Dad, it doesn't bear thinking about. Did you know Ruby Armstrong? I mean did you know her well enough to sum up what she was like as a person? Did she strike you as the sort of girl who would just clear off without saying a word? Her mother's a widow, you know.'

Matthew sat down heavily on the side of the double bed, so heavily that the box-spring mattress creaked in protest. Then he eased his feet out of his black shoes and into a pair of tartan house slippers. 'That's better, by heck. I try, lass. I try to keep tabs on all my weavers, but it's not like it were when your grandad ran the mill. He had time to take a fatherly interest in all of them, but it's as much as I can do to keep up with the administration side these days. As much as I can do to keep the looms running full time.' He stroked his chin. 'Aye, things have changed, and not for the better.' He put up a warning finger, then smiled. 'Thought I heard your mother coming up, but she's on the telephone. To your Auntie Ethel I shouldn't wonder. About this 'ere wedding.'

'The hat,' Dorothy said, and they smiled and nodded at each other.

'About this Ruby Armstrong girl, chuck. I can tell you one thing, and that is she's a good and quick worker. A bit of a different cup of tea from some of the other weavers. Not always shouting and shrieking to her mates all day.' He undid the top button of his trousers for further comfort. 'I remember like it were yesterday her mother bringing her to

46

see me about two years ago when she first started in the weaving shed. Aye, she'd be about fourteen, just left school. I can see her now, standing there in the office in her navy-blue school mac, all big-eyed and shy, with her mother doing all the talking. More or less telling me that if I didn't look after her daughter she'd give me what for. Nice woman though. Just lost her husband. But a bit of a tiger. Wanting the best for her kids all along the line.'

'Stanley's won a state scholarship to Oxford,' Dorothy said, the pride in her voice giving her away. 'He's really clever, Dad. Special clever. You know?'

Matthew patted a place beside him on the bed.

'Special to *you*, love?'

Dorothy swallowed, hoping to avoid the hated blush. It worked sometimes, but not this time. 'I think so, Dad. We can talk, you know? Really say things that matter to each other, though we argue a lot of the time. He's always on the side of the under-dog.' She smiled. 'He says you're a bloated capitalist.'

Matthew roared with laughter. 'Does he now? Doesn't he know that's what he'll be when he's finished at yon university, and got himself a good job? There's nowt like a bit of education and a few letters behind a man's name for turning a Bolshie into one of us. You ask him if he'll be prepared to work along o' the masses when he can put them letters behind his name? I've seen many a man join the ranks of what he had considered to be the privileged, when education lifts him up amongst them.'

'He's not a Bolshie,' Dorothy said quickly. 'He just wants a better deal for everybody, regardless of creed, colour or class.'

'There were a chap called Jesus who wanted that,' Matthew said with a grim smile. 'But it don't work in practice, love. There'll always be them what comes out of the top drawer, and them what stays in the bottom. I'd like to meet this lad of yours sometime, but your mother worries about you, love. Some day, when you have kids of your

47

own, you'll understand. That Mrs Armstrong and your mother, they're both tarred with the same brush, you know, if you think about it. Both wanting the best for their children, be it three looms in a weaving shed, or a place at university, or a husband who's passed his accountancy exams and talks posh.'

'You like Gerald, don't you, Dad?'

Dorothy's voice was no more than a whisper as she heard the telephone being replaced on its hook downstairs.

'Aye, I like him. He knows his job, I'll say that for him, though I've always felt that chaps who work with figures and the balancing of them are bound to be double dealers in a certain kind of way. All them accounts to make come out right, they're bound to push them one way or t'other if you think about it. He makes our Margaret happy, and he makes your mother happy, and that's all that matters it seems to me.'

Dorothy leaned up against him. 'You're a right softie, did you know that, Dad?'

He dropped a kiss on her hair. 'Get away with you, love. But think on what I've said now, and don't go getting yourself all involved before you've had time to grow up and see what other fish there might be in the sea first. All right?'

She smiled into his cardigan. 'And how many times has Mother told me that you and her were childhood sweethearts? That neither of you had ever known anyone else?'

'There were a war on, love, and I was sent to France right at the beginning. Things were different.'

'Of course,' said Dorothy.

'Matthew?' Phyllis's voice spiralled upstairs with more than a touch of hysteria in it. 'Can you come down a minute? I've just been talking to the man at The Pied Bull about the reception, and he says the room we've booked can't take more than seventy-five.'

Matthew got to his feet and shrugged his shoulders. 'Coming love. I'll nobbut be more than a minute.'

Then he put a hand on Dorothy's shoulder. 'Try and be

48

happy, love. That's all I want for you in the long run, and your mother too, if you could but realize it. This Ruby girl – she'll turn up, you'll see. Things have a way of turning out right, and this boy . . . remember he's got years of study in front of him, and you don't want to be missing out on all the fun you could be having by waiting for him or anything daft like that. Take my word for it, he'll change, and you'll change.' He walked towards the door. 'Let it slide, love. Just let it be till you're both old enough to know your own minds. You won't believe me now, but there's no hurry. No hurry at all.'

'Matthew!'

'Seems like there is!' he said, winking broadly at his daughter before he left the room.

Dorothy, alone in her room, with the sound of rain spattering the tall windows, and a wind sighing in the tall elm tree at the bottom of the back garden, tried to care whether Cromwell had been a good leader, and failed. What was the point in swotting for a Higher School Certificate she wasn't going to take anyway? And how could she possibly concentrate on events that had happened three hundred years ago when what was happening now filled every corner of her mind? If only Stanley was on the telephone, she could ring him and find out. If only she'd asked him to slip out somehow and ring *her*. '*Oliver Cromwell was a man of the people*,' she wrote then chewed the end of her pen and stared at the wallpaper until the triangles filled with baskets of flowers went out of focus.

At twenty past nine she went downstairs and joined her parents in the lounge.

Matthew turned to her with the smile that always lit his face whenever she came into a room. 'Want me to keep the wireless on, love? The talk's finished but it's Jack Hylton's band on next. You like him, don't you?'

'I don't mind,' she said, in such a dispirited way that her

mother laid her knitting down in her lap for a moment, and raised her eyes ceilingwards as if searching for patience.

Dorothy flopped down in a corner of the huge chintz-covered chesterfield. 'I am an awful worry to her,' she thought, with a sudden flash of perception. 'There's no communication between us at all. I can't play the part she wants me to play therefore we have nothing of consequence to say to each other. I am driving her mad tonight because I can't stop wondering what's going on in Inkerman Street, and I can't tell her the reason for my restlessness because I couldn't bear the things she'd say.'

Matthew hadn't told his wife about the missing weaver either. He shifted in his chair . . . Was he frightened of his own wife, or summat? Nay, never say that. But what he didn't want, after the long and tiring day at the mill, was a long discussion on Dorothy's friendship with yon poor lass's brother. He knew his Phyllis, and the mystery of the lost girl would be as nothing compared with the fact that Dorothy was involved, even indirectly.

'Love is the sweetest thing,' the band on the wireless was playing, and he couldn't resist giving his daughter a wink. Nay, dammit, what was more normal than thinking you were in love at seventeen? Maybe he was an abnormal father or something? He'd read somewhere that fathers were supposed to be jealous of their daughters' sweethearts. Well, all he could say was that he would be right glad to see both of them nicely married off. In white, of course, to please Phyllis, with him all dressed up in a top hat and tails like Sunny Jim on a packet of Force cereal, if that was the way she wanted it. . . .

'Sitting like that, slid down in your chair, is giving you a big stomach, Matthew,' she was saying now, so pretending he hadn't heard her, he closed his eyes and crossed his hands over the offending part of his anatomy. Dashed if he'd let a woman tell him how to sit in his own chair, his closed and shuttered expression said.

'I think I'll go up and have a bath,' Dorothy said, jumping up quickly and leaving the room before her mother could ask her please not to take all the hot water, as she never failed to do.

'What's the matter with her tonight?' she heard Phyllis ask before she got to the foot of the wide oak staircase.

Followed by her father's answering murmur, 'Leave her be, love. Just leave her be. . . .'

And she was lying back in the warm scented water when she heard the telephone ringing in the hall, and her father's measured tread as he went to answer it. She tried to hear what he was saying, and it was impossible, but he wasn't on long, and as she climbed out of the bath and started to dry herself, she heard a tap on the bathroom door.

'It's me, love,' her father said, and something in the sound of his voice made her wind the big pink towel round her body, tucking it in above her breasts. She opened the door and knew even as she saw his face that what she had been dreading had happened.

'It was the station, love,' Matthew told her, his red face redder than ever with concern for her. 'Now I don't want you going and upsetting yoursen, but I did promise to tell you the minute I heard owt.'

'They've found her, haven't they?' Dorothy bowed her head and stared down at her bare feet.

'It was Sergeant Bates, chuck. He promised to let me know.'

'Tell me, Dad.'

Matthew sighed, wanting to spare her, but knowing that he couldn't. 'Aye, they've found her body, love.' Then he reached for her and held her close, just as if she were a child again and he'd come up the stairs to rub her dry.

'She were in the Corporation Park. Strangled by the looks of her, the sergeant said. They've sent a man round to tell her mother . . . Aye, it's a bad business all right.'

Dorothy's voice came muffled from his shoulder.

51

'Where in the park, Father?'

Matthew turned his head and saw his wife coming along the landing. He shook his head at her. 'Keep out of this, please,' his expression said.

'By the duck pond, chuck. Hidden beneath a rhododendron bush. Seems a courting couple trying to shelter from the rain stumbled over something . . . Now then, hold up, love. Come on now, let's get you to your room and into bed.' He patted her shoulder with small comforting gestures.

But Dorothy was past comfort, past noticing or even caring that the pink towel was slipping down exposing one rounded breast. Her heart was pounding so loudly she felt she would suffocate with the sound of it.

'Oh, no! Oh no . . . I was talking to Stanley this afternoon in the park. We were sitting on the bench where we always sit, one of the benches near to the duck pond. We could have been sitting right where . . .' She raised an anguished face. 'Stanley was late, and then when he came he told me that Ruby hadn't come home all night. And all the time we were talking she could have been lying not far away. Perhaps not more than a few yards from us. He was actually telling me that she was missing, and all the time . . . Oh God! She might even have been alive. And we just sat there . . .'

Her voice rose high, wavering on the verge of lost control. Matthew shook her gently.

'She wasn't alive, lovey. Now stop torturing yourself with thoughts like that. You're letting that imagination of yours run away with itself again.' He was guiding her slowly along the wide landing as he talked to her in his flat voice, his northern accent becoming more pronounced as his concern for her increased.

'She were *dead*, chuck. There were nowt you could have done even if you'd found her. Now, come on, be a good girl and get into bed.'

Dorothy started to whimper, 'I've got to go to Stanley.

I'm his friend, and he'll want to see me. I can't just go to bed, I can't. Oh, Dad, how could anyone do that to a girl like Ruby Armstrong? She was so pretty. I've seen Gerald and Mr Sowerbutts talking to her down at the mill. Everyone liked her. They did, didn't they? She was a *good* girl. She didn't mess about with boys, Stanley told me. She'd only been out with the boy next door ... oh ... her poor mother ...'

'Into bed, love.' Matthew motioned to his wife and nodded at the blue nightdress lying over the foot of the bed.

'Help her into that, lass, then go down and make a pot of tea. Strong and with plenty of sugar in it. I'll stay here.'

And for once in her life, Phyllis Bolton didn't argue. . . .

Matthew tucked his daughter into her bed, and pulled the satin eiderdown up round her shoulders. Her face was the colour of putty, and her eyes were staring at him, trying to make him understand.

'Take me down to Stanley's house, Dad. Please.'

He shook his head firmly. 'It wouldn't be right, love. Now listen to me. It's not the time for anyone else to be there, not tonight. This is a private time, both for Stanley and his mother. The police will be as kind as they know how to be, but there'll be things, unpleasant things to be done.' He hesitated, then went on: 'Someone will have to identify the . . . the body, and there'll be more questions. I doubt if anyone down there will see their beds tonight.' He knelt down awkwardly and took her hands in his own, squeezing them gently, trying to soothe, at a loss to know what to say, wondering just how far things had gone between his Dorothy and this boy, this *special* boy who would have to be more than a son to his mother this night.

'I'll take you in the morning,' he said, unable to bear the pleading in her eyes. 'First thing. I'll want to let Mrs Armstrong know that I'll help her in any way I can, and you can come with me. First thing.'

From downstairs came the sound of light voices in the hall, and the sound of Margaret's laughter, suddenly switched off as Phyllis told them what had happened.

Dorothy raised herself on one elbow, her blue eyes wide with distress. 'Don't let them come upstairs, Dad. Don't let them come near me. I couldn't bear to talk to them just now.'

'There'll nobody come near you, love,' Matthew said, rising stiffly from his knees and taking a cup of tea from Margaret as she started to walk into the room.

'Gerald wants to know if there's anything . . .' she began, and the look on her face turned to one of astonishment as her father turned her round and pushed her none too gently from the room.

'Tell Gerald . . . oh tell him to push off,' he said firmly and closed the door.

Five

The policeman stopped under a street lamp half way up Inkerman Street. Its yellow beam showed the serious set of his pointed features and the rain glistening on the folds of his cape. 'No use in stopping, Albert,' he told himself. 'What has to be done has to be done.' Then he walked with a heavy tread further up the street and knocked three times on the door of number twenty-seven.

By God, did it never do owt else but rain in this damned town? And what was he doing standing here? He ought to be going to bed like all the other occupants of the street. He glanced at the lighted upstairs windows and saw a face appear from behind the drawn curtains of the house directly opposite. Aye, the happenings of the day had given them something to talk about right enough. Something to take their minds off the dole queues and the worry for some of them as to where the next meal was coming from. He knocked again. . . .

When he heard the footsteps coming down the passage towards the door, he wished he could just turn and walk away. Run away, he meant really. Back down the sloping street with its flagstones glistening with rain, back to his own little semi-detached house out on the Manchester side of the town, where his wife would be waiting with a pint pot of cocoa, and the fire burning in the grate, and his new-born son asleep upstairs in his cot. Back to sanity, and back to normality.

The door opened, and the young man who stood back to

let him pass looked as if he hadn't slept for days. His eyes were bloodshot and sunk deep in his face – two dark holes that looked as if they'd been chiselled out of his flesh. He didn't speak, just preceded him down the darkened passage into the light of a living-room, where a woman sat by the fire, so still she might have been growing there.

The policeman took his helmet off and held it underneath his arm. 'Mrs Armstrong?'

'Aye.' Her voice was no more than a whisper.

He had to say it. Quickly too, there being no way of softening a blow like this. No way of leading up to it nicely. . . .

'Mrs Armstrong. I'm afraid I've brought bad news. We've found your daughter's body in the Corporation Park. At least her clothes and her description fit.' He turned to Stanley, the poor woman obviously having failed to take in what he was saying. 'I'd like you to come with me, lad, to make the necessary indentification.'

There, it was said, and oh, dear God, who in hell's name would want to be a policeman? This was a far cry from taking down details of lost cats and dogs, picking up Friday night drunks out of the gutter. They were both staring at him as if they hated his guts, as if it were his fault or something. If one of them didn't speak he'd have to say it all over again. He put the helmet down on the table. 'Mrs Armstrong?'

Then, to his horror, the still brooding statue of the little woman came to life. Making a sound like a kicked-in-the-belly animal, she put a hand over her mouth, got to her feet and ran out of the over-heated room.

He heard her retching and vomiting out in the back scullery, an abandoned sound, terrible in its lack of dignity, awesome in its total despair.

The boy standing by the table turned to follow her.

'I'll just go . . .' he said over his shoulder, and the policeman took a handkerchief from his pocket and wiped the rain and perspiration from his face.

'If she wants . . .' he began, but Stanley was already by his mother's side, watching helplessly as she vomited, then in between the bouts of vomiting, banged her head again and again on the stone slopstone.

To the end of his days he was never to forget the terrible sound of her forehead being dashed over and over on the unyielding stone. Banging, banging away in a frenzy of disbelief, as if she would knock the truth out of her mind, her active brain a riot of confusion.

'Mum . . .' he said, and tried to put his arms round her, but she knocked him away with a force that made him stagger back and clutch at the gas-stove to keep his balance.

'Mum! You'll hurt yourself.'

'No!' she was shouting. 'I'll not believe it. I'll not. Tell him to go away with his lies. Ruby's not dead. She'll come back home. I'll not listen to him. I'll not listen.'

Then she straightened up, turned around, and put both hands over her face, and as Stanley reached for her, he saw the blood running down between her fingers.

Dazed, moaning with a dreadful whimpering sound, his mother swayed, temporarily out of her mind with grief. Making no further protest when the policeman came and led her gently back to her chair by the fire. Kneeling by her side and wiping the blood from her head with his white handkerchief.

'Is there a neighbour, lad? A woman who could come in and be with her?' He spoke softly over his shoulder to Stanley.

'Mrs Crawley. I'll go and fetch her . . . It's only across the street, only a minute. I'll not be a minute . . .'

And reaching the front door, Stanley almost pulled it off its hinges with the force he used to get it open quickly enough.

'What can Mrs Crawley do?' a voice in his head seemed to be screaming over and over. He was not and never had been a swearer, his father having instilled in him the belief that there were enough words in the English language

57

without needing to curse, but now the voice was shouting: 'What can bloody Mrs Crawley do? What can *anyone* do?'

And they'd gone to bed. He could see the light on upstairs. What right had they being in bed when his mother needed, when his mother. . . ? Stanley banged on the door as if the very hounds of hell were hard on his heels.

'Mrs Crawley! Mrs Crawley . . .'

But it was Mr Crawley who answered the door. Undersized, shrivelled little Mr Crawley, with his indefinite features set anonymously in his forgettable face; a man so dominated by his wife that he hardly seemed to exist. He blinked at Stanley, and screwed up his face as if trying to place him. Half way through undressing for bed, he was trying to pull his dangling braces back over his shoulders, making ineffectual little grabs at them.

''Old on, lad. There's no call for thee to try to break door down.' Then he saw Stanley's face. 'Eh, lad, I didn't know it were thee. Come in with ee. I'll get 'er.' He went to the foot of the stairs, and shouted with surprising strength in his voice. 'Nellie! It's yon lad from across street.' He turned back to Stanley. 'Nay, lad. Come in out of the wet. It's a nasty neet all right.'

And moving like a machine, Stanley stepped inside.

Within minutes Mrs Crawley was there, the saviour of Inkerman Street, clattering her way down the uncarpeted stairs, with a coat thrown over a grey and trailing nightdress, her hair a-bristle with curling pins, and her sunken mouth proclaiming that her teeth were reposing elsewhere for the night.

'They've found her,' Stanley heard himself say. 'In the park. Me mum . . . oh, Mrs Crawley, can you come? I've got to go with the policeman, and she can't be left by herself.'

'Aye,' Nellie Crawley said, and started off down the lobby just as she was, leaving her husband hovering silently and uncertainly in the background.

'She might do herself an injury,' Stanley told her, as they

crossed the darkened street together. He looked up in apparent surprise to feel the rain on his face. 'But it's Ruby all right. They had a description of the clothes she was wearing.'

Mrs Crawley tripped over the kerb, and as Stanley put out an arm to support her he caught the smell of spirits on her breath.

'Poor bloody little sod,' she said, and he felt that his father would have understood.

'Aye, there's some bad buggers, there are 'n all,' Nellie said, pushing open the door of number twenty-seven, and stepping inside.

Apart from the deep purple bruises on her throat, Ruby Armstrong might have been sleeping. Her face had a waxen quality about it, and there was a leaf caught up in her dark curly hair.

Still moving as if in a dream, Stanley gently picked it out and let it fall to the ground.

'This is your sister? Ruby Armstrong?' The police sergeant's voice was quiet and filled with compassion. Nay, God damn it, he had a daughter at home about the same age as this poor lass. His fingers trembled as he held the sheet aloft. It didn't bear thinking about.

Stanley nodded. 'It's her all right.' Then, before the sheet fell into place over that still face, he touched the pale face gently.

'Goodbye, Ruby,' he said foolishly, and turned away.

And when it was over the police sergeant said they would see him home, but Stanley shook his head.

'It's not far.'

And the trams were still running, lumbering and rocking along the lines, dropping passengers in the middle of the road beneath their spider's web of wires. People were going home from the second-house pictures, peering through the steamed-up windows, rubbing at the glass with their hands.

The same people who would read of Ruby's death in the papers the next morning, gloat over the details, shudder when they thought for a tingling moment that it might have been them; might have been their daughter.

Stanley walked on, shoulders hunched, hands thrust deep in his pockets, slouching along, like one of the great army of unemployed, with all hope gone. But now his despair was even more terrible than theirs. Heedless of the rain soaking his dark hair, flattening it to his skull, thinking of his father, and remembering how Ruby had run down the street to meet him when he came home from work every evening at half-past five.

Thinking what his dad would have done to the man who had done this unbelievable, terrible thing.

Harry Armstrong had been a quiet man, not given to rages or violent turn of speech, but it seemed to Stanley as if he was there, walking beside him now, his thin face blazing with murderous anger.

'I'll swing for him that did it, so help me God,' he was saying, and his words found an ache in his son's heart and mind.

'Mum,' he promised, muttering to himself as he turned the corner into Inkerman Street, 'I'll not rest until they find him. I'll give up the scholarship, and work and stay with you. I'll find work somewhere. Anywhere. Just so long as I'm with you. It was all a bit too much like a dream anyway, me going to Oxford. You'll have to forget it, Mum. It just wasn't meant to be . . . that's all.'

Matthew stayed with Dorothy until she slept, a twitching sleep induced by weeping, and a subconscious desire, he guessed, to escape from the realization of what had happened. Tomorrow she would be as calm as a canal on a summer's day. That had always been Dorothy's way. Flying into storms of crying, getting it all over and done with, then settling down to the inevitable. He sighed and made his way downstairs to where his wife and Margaret were sitting over a dying fire, the sherry decanter on the coffee table between them.

'Gerald's gone,' Margaret said, looking at her father with a hurt look on her face, remembering what he'd said upstairs, but making allowances for him.

'He talked very sensibly,' Phyllis said, 'and he's coming to pick Margaret up in the morning, because he thought you would most likely be wanting to go down and see that poor girl's mother. He can't get over it,' she added, staring down at the glass in her hands. 'We were going to make a pot of tea, but we felt like something stronger, didn't we, Margaret?'

'You never think a thing like this could happen in your own circle.'

Phyllis gave her elder daughter a swift glance. 'Well, not exactly in our own circle, dear, but I know what you mean. I expect you *will* have to go down there in the morning, Matthew?'

Matthew sat down in his chair, and rubbed his receding forehead wearily with the back of his hand. 'Aye, I'll be going down first thing. It's the least I can do.' He looked his wife straight in the eye. 'And I'll be taking Dorothy with me. Seems she's been seeing a lot more of that lad than we realized, and telling us lies all along the line.' Like that poor dead lass was telling *her* mother lies, he thought, shaking his head. 'From what she's told me I gather she's pretty fond of him – they met and talked this afternoon, not more than a few yards away from where they found the body. Now you know why she was so upset.' He sighed. 'Our Dorothy's a bit too young and a sight too vulnerable to cope with a situation like that. She's going to need all our understanding for the next few days; you know how she takes things too much to heart, always has.'

Phyllis exchanged a glance with Margaret, but before she could say anything, Matthew went on: 'Now lass, this isn't the time to quibble. The right or wrongs of whether she should have been meeting him on the sly don't seem to matter. Quibble now, make an issue out of it now and she's not likely to forgive us. Ever.'

His wife took a dainty sip from the sherry glass. 'All I was going to say, Matthew, *when* you give me a chance to speak, was that I feel sure you don't want Dorothy *involved* in this dreadful affair any more than I do.' She took another sip. 'I agree with you that she takes things very much to heart, coupled with this intense loyalty she has towards her friends, but I feel strongly that this time she needs protecting against herself.'

Margaret nodded, and Matthew knew that they had been discussing ways and means of making him see what they thought was sound sense. 'I never meant it that way,' he thought, 'but here we are, here we've always been, two sides. Me and Dorothy on the one side, and Margaret and her mother on the other.'

'There'll be reporters, Father, and you know what they can be like. You're involved already with the poor girl working at the mill, but once they find out that Dorothy is friendly with the brother, can't you imagine what they'll make out of it? There hasn't been a murder case they could get their teeth into for ages, apart from the two unsolved ones out Barnoldswick way.'

'Four years ago,' Phyllis said, 'there was a woman in Agincourt Street who killed her husband with the coal shovel when he came home from the public house one night. Too drunk to defend himself, they said.' She sniffed. 'Agincourt Street's round the corner from Inkerman Street, isn't it?'

The inference was deliberate, and Matthew felt his throat contract with a kind of pain. All right then, he was allowing himself to get emotionally involved already; he was caring too much, but if the alternative was to sit there sipping sherry and calmly thinking out ways and means of disconnecting yourself from what had happened – well, he knew the way he'd choose to be. God damn it, people were *people*, weren't they, regardless of whether they come from Agincourt Street or Buckingham Palace? He found he was clenching his fists so that the nails dug into the palms of his hands. . . .

'This is a young and decent girl who has been brutally murdered,' he said, trying to control the pitch of his voice. Phyllis was always accusing him of talking too loud. 'It could have been you, Margaret. Or Dorothy. Aye, it might well have been our Dorothy as it seems she's been meeting this lad in the park every day after school.' He gave up the attempt to speak quietly. 'And do you know why she's been meeting him in the park, in a secluded place, on the sly, then? Because she knew she couldn't bring him back to this house. Because every time she tried to mention his name her mother's nose wrinkled as if there were a bad smell under it. Because she wasn't prepared to face the schemozzle of bringing her friendship out into the open. That's why.'

Phyllis put her glass down on the low table, saw that it had left a ring, and took it up again to wipe the rounded base with her handkerchief. 'I expect, Matthew,' she said, obviously determined to keep her own voice low to show the difference, 'I expect you have conveniently forgotten that if this poor young girl's mother had been more concerned about the company her daughter had been keeping, this ghastly thing might never have happened? At least Dorothy knows that we disapprove of her meeting this young man, and this, this dreadful thing that's happened, may show her that we could have been right.'

'You mean that murders don't happen in the best of circles?'

'I mean, Matthew, that the young girl in question probably had a far different set of values from the ones we've set our two girls. They think differently, and you know that's true. They live in these hard times by a system of a communal pooling of their wages, no planning, no system. Why, during the General Strike a friend of mine told me that the miner's wives were dressed like middle-class women.'

63

Now Matthew really lost his temper. 'What in the name of thunder are you talking about woman? No wonder there's bloody revolutions! What the hell have the miners' wives in the Strike got to do with what we're talking about?'

Phyllis was quite unruffled. 'Then there's the wedding to think about.' She smiled a small tight smile. 'It wouldn't look good now, would it, if the chief bridesmaid was pointed out as the girl who was friendly with that boy whose sister was murdered in the Corporation Park? You have a certain position to keep in the town, Matthew, and things get twisted. People *exaggerate*.'

Matthew could take no more. Going over to the sideboard, he took out a bottle of whisky. He got to the door and came back for a glass. 'I'm going to bed, lass. Otherwise I might be tempted to say something I might be sorry for.' He turned, the bottle swinging from his podgy fingers. 'And in the morning, Dorothy's coming with me when I go to see that poor widow woman.' More telling words failed him . . . 'So put that in your pipe and smoke it,' he said, closing the door none too gently behind him.

But when Phyllis came up to bed ten minutes later, the whisky he'd drunk had done no more than soften his mood. Made him see both sides of the pictures, the way he always did when confronted with a problem at the mill. It had been this quality, recognized by his influential friends years ago, that had made them try to persuade him to let his name go forward as a potential magistrate, and perhaps paradoxically it had been this very quality that had made him refuse.

'Nay, but I'd be no good at playing God,' he'd said. 'And besides I haven't the time to spend sitting on my backside on the Bench. Nay, leave that to them what've got themselves sorted out better than what I have.'

And in somebody's book, Phyllis was a good woman, a marvellous hostess and a conscientious mother. No doubt about that. So, seeing her set face, and sensing her air of injured martyrdom, he put his arm round her when she got into bed beside him. 'I know you mean well, lass. You always do, especially when it comes to thinking what's best for the girls. But this is something far more important than worrying what folks might think. And even a local murder's a nine days' wonder, don't forget. Come June and the wedding, and it will all be a thing of the past. The police will catch the man who did it, and that will be that. But our Dorothy will find it hard to forgive you if you try to stop her standing by a friend at a time like this. Other folks might forget the murder, but she'll never forget your attitude.' He tried to pull her closer to him, and kissed her clumsily on her cheek.

'The smell of whisky makes me feel sick,' Phyllis said, but she didn't turn over, and he knew that for the time being he had won. For the time being at least. . . .

There was only a tiny mention of the murder in the *Manchester Guardian* when he picked it up off the mat early the next morning, but the *Daily Mail* had spent a hectic night scrapping its first page, and had printed the details in banner headlines.

YOUNG MILL GIRL BRUTALLY MURDERED, it said, and Matthew sighed. This would put the cat among the pigeons all right. Heavens knew what the *News of the World* would make of it on Sunday when more details had been released by the police. He could see it now, with a photograph of Ruby Armstrong's three looms in the weaving shed, and on-the-spot interviews with her mates. He imagined the excitement it would bring into *their* drab lives, with every one of them claiming to be the dead girl's best pal.

He took the papers up into the bathroom with him whilst he shaved, in what he knew was a vain attempt to prevent Phyllis seeing them. He wished, not for the first time since he had married, that his wife was the kind of woman who stayed in bed till he'd got off to work. But that wasn't Phyllis's way at all.

The routine never varied. He had the use of the bathroom first, whilst she washed at the wash-stand in the bathroom. Then Margaret and Dorothy took turns in the bathroom, and by the time they got downstairs, Phyllis was there, fully dressed in tweed skirt and jumper, pearl ear-rings screwed into the lobes of her ears, and her immaculate hair and the red mark across her forehead proclaiming to the discerning that she had slept the night securely enmeshed in a hair-net.

It was orderly, organized, and calculated to send a man off to his work with the feeling that, whatever the day in front of him might bring, the start to his day had been as devoid of stress as a paddle in the sea at Blackpool.

But this was no ordinary day. He winced as the razor slipped and nicked a piece out of his chin, then with a strip of lavatory paper sticking to the small cut, he walked back along the wide landing to his room, with the bed already turned down ready for Mrs Wilkinson's ministrations, and the bottle of whisky, and the glass he'd used, taken away, so that it could never be said that Mr Bolton drank in bed. . . .

And Dorothy was pale, but composed, just as he had prophesied she would be, and Margaret was late sitting down at the table, having spent longer on her face and her hair than usual. Phyllis was determinedly saying nothing.

'Two strong wills out to please themselves,' she had told the bacon as she flipped it over in the frying-pan. Two rashers each, with the eggs broken into a cup first. 'So what is the point of *me* saying anything?' Besides, Gerald was coming round to pick Margaret up, and heaven forbid that he would think they were the sort of family who made bother over the breakfast table. He had hinted vaguely about having had a nanny when he was a small boy.

'I can just imagine him as a dear little red-haired Christopher Robin, can't you?' she had asked her sister Ethel, who had gone home and told her husband Raymond that she thought Phyllis was getting carried away.

'You'd think their Margaret was marrying into royalty,' she'd sniffed.

He rang the bell just as Phyllis was carrying the plates through into the dining-room.

'That smells good, Mrs Bolton,' he said, smiling.

He was wearing a suit she hadn't seen before in a dark blue cloth, with a matching waistcoat, and his hair, flattened to his head with brilliantine, shone a darker red in the sunshine streaming through the high window in the hall. Margaret, who had let him in, kissed him on his closely shaven cheek, and thought he looked and smelled delicious.

'Don't tease Dorothy this morning,' she whispered to him. 'You've seen it in the paper about the beastly park murder? You remember I told you she was friendly with the girl's brother? Well, Father is taking her with him when he goes to the house. Mother and him had words about it last night.'

'Beastly business all right,' Gerald said, and followed her into the dining-room.

'Cup of tea, Gerald?'

Phyllis raised the pot and smiled at him. 'I do believe we might be getting some warmer weather at last. It says on the wireless that it's going to rain later, but I refuse to believe it.'

Gerald shook his head. 'No tea for me, thank you, Mrs Bolton. I'll just sit here and look at the papers if you don't mind.' And he took them from the sideboard where Matthew had hoped they might lie until he'd left the house.

'Aye, it's in,' he said, in answer to his wife's raised eyebrows. 'Trust the *Mail* to be quickest off the mark.'

'Beastly business,' Gerald said, reading the account avidly as they ate. 'Don't feel you have to hurry back to the mill, Mr Bolton. I can cope with anything that might crop up, and fob the police off if they try to disrupt things too much.'

Matthew smiled wryly, wondering what old Tom Sowerbutts, who had worked at the mill as under-manager since

67

his father's time, would have to say to that. Wondered, not for the first time, if Tom's decision to retire at the end of the year had anything to with the arrival of the young accountant from London.

'New brooms sweep clean, Mr Bolton,' he'd said when Gerald's method had clashed with his own well-tried schemes. 'And never let it be said that I clung on when my time came to go. Besides, the wife and me have set our minds on a bungalow at St. Annes. It'll be nice for the grandchildren to come and spend their school holidays with us – all them sand-dunes to play hide-and-seek in, and Blackpool not more than a tram ride away.'

'We won't be stopping down Inkerman Street, just calling there,' Matthew told Gerald. 'It's just the least I can do to offer to help in any way I can.' He folded his white starched napkin up and rolled it into the right shape for the silver ring. 'Finished, Dorothy, love?'

And in spite of his warning glances, Phyllis followed them to the door, handing her husband his trilby, and telling Dorothy to come straight back with Philips in the car.

'I won't feel safe with you out on the streets till they've caught that man,' she said, and flushed as Dorothy gave her an unexpected kiss on the cheek.

'Thanks a lot, Mother, for not going on about it. If I . . . if I can see that I'm in the way, I won't even go in . . . it's just that I want Stanley to know that I'm . . . that I . . .'

Phyllis counted ten to stop herself from saying that surely a nicely worded letter would have done just as well, but in any case Mrs Wilkinson was coming up the path clutching the inevitable basket, and whatever Phyllis might have said was certainly not for *her* ears.

And to anyone walking down the tree-lined road that spring morning, with the sunshine lying dappled on the wide pavement, and with Philips holding the door of the car open as his employer and his daughter climbed in, there was nothing to suggest that life in the big house wasn't going on in its usual serene way.

'Good morning, Mrs Bolton,' Mrs Wilkinson said as she made her way round the back of the house to the side door.

'Good morning, Mrs Wilkinson,' Phyllis answered, waving as the car reversed into the road.

Then she closed the door and walked into the kitchen where Mrs Wilkinson was tying the strings of her flowered apron behind her back, and saw the *Daily Express* reposing in the basket on top of the fur-trimmed bedroom slippers.

'That poor little lass,' Mrs Wilkinson said, sitting down on a kitchen chair to ease her feet out of her bunion-shaped black lace-ups. 'To think that your Dorothy is so friendly with her brother! It brings it home don't it? – when you actually know the family what's involved. I could see how pale she was, poor lass, she must be right cut up about it. Did she know the sister – the one what's been murdered – as well?'

Phyllis closed her eyes for a moment. It was beginning already. . . .

Six

'You've been to Stanley's house before, have you, love?' Matthew Bolton's voice was gentle. This was not the time for recriminations, or even for questions, and the way he phrased it made it sound more like a statement of fact.

Dorothy shook her head. She looked scared half way to death, as if what she was doing was a tactless embarrassment, but had to be done all the same. Like strangers gatecrashing somebody's funeral, Matthew thought grimly. He patted her knee.

'I'm not trying to pry, chuck.'

She forced a smile. 'I know that, Father, but Stanley's mother knows about me. She's told him off many a time for not being more open about being friendly with me. She asked him was he ashamed of me, or something?'

Matthew's mouth turned up at the corner. Aye, he could just imagine Mrs Armstrong saying that. She would see nowt wrong with her son being friendly with, or courting, a mill owner's daughter. She'd reckon her Stanley was doing Dorothy a favour . . . he'd come up against that fierce kind of pride many a time in his dealings with his workers at the mill. He didn't suppose Ada Armstrong would turn a hair of her black head if her Stanley took the King's daughter back for tea. And that was something Phyllis would *never* understand. Pride to her was based on possessions – what a man had, not what he was. Change a man's accent and his mode of dress and his status in life matched. Nay, Phyllis would never understand. He breathed deeply, staring straight forward, transfixed, at nothing. What was it his father used to say?

'Do what's right, lad, and there's no one in the whole world better than thee. Allus remember that.'

They were turning now into Marston Road, a long road with the houses, though terraced, of Victorian respectability. Each with its own flight of steps, some of them made of dark red and yellow tiles, adding a note of almost Continental cheerfulness. Here lived the white-collar workers of the town. The clerks, the shop managers, the printers and compositors, with unleafing bushes in the tiny iron-railed front gardens, and if they were lucky, the box-room plumbed in as a bathroom. Matthew was pleased to see that Dorothy was leaning forward, staring out of the car window with interest. Seeing how the other half live, Phyllis would have said.

'Do you know, I've never been along here before? Isn't that awful? I've lived here all my life and I've never even been this way.'

The part of her that was all Phyllis was deciding privately that these houses weren't bad at all. One of them had a striped awning over the front door, almost a replica of the one Philips would be fitting over their own polished front door, should the sun shine for more than two days running.

But Philips was signalling right now and turning the car into a much narrower street, and there, far below them, was a panoramic view of the town, its thousands of chimney pots on thousands of roofs lit to a mellow softness by the early morning sun, its tall mill chimneys pointing black fingers into the blue sky.

Here, as the car moved slowly down the steep slope, the houses huddled closely together, front doors opening straight on to flagged pavements. Women, down on their knees on pieces of matting, were mopping doorsteps, edging them with a thick line of yellow-stone, wiping over a semi-circle of flags directly in front of their own door. Throwing pails of water over the entire frontage, then

71

sweeping the water into the gutter with long-handled brushes. Standing on straight-backed chairs to clean the windows with wash-leather bundles, the more daring sitting out of the top windows, clinging on with one hand and feverishly rubbing away with the other.

'It's the next street, Mr Bolton.'

The back of Philips's neck betrayed his ill-concealed excitement at what was going on, by taking on the hue of a ripe tomato. After all, as he was to tell Vera that evening, going to the house of a murder victim was not the sort of thing everybody did every day. It had upset him, of course it had, but all the same, there was a sense of importance and even of excitement at being involved, even if only indirectly. Like all the people who had claimed to be patients of Dr Crippen. . . . He shuddered pleasurably.

But if Philips had been expecting to have to beat off crowds of reporters, or avid sightseers round the door of 27 Inkerman Street, he was doomed to disappointment. Death was respected and given its fair due in streets like Inkerman Street. Now that it was common knowledge that Ruby Armstrong was dead, the flag-moppers and step-stoners were at the backs of their houses, doing their gossiping over the yard walls, or standing in little groups beneath the lines of flapping washing in the cobbled backs. Front doors were closed, and some of the neighbours, in a gesture of sympathy, had drawn their long curtains, giving the short steep street a closed and shuttered appearance.

Philips parked the black car at the kerb, and before he could get out to open the rear door, was told to stay where he was.

'We'll not be long,' Matthew said, holding out his hand to Dorothy. Then, crossing the pavement, he raised the iron knocker set high in the door of twenty-seven, and gave three short raps.

'I won't know what to say . . .'

Dorothy turned a worried face towards him, looking, at that moment, far younger than her seventeen years. 'To say

72

we're sorry seems so . . . so inadequate.'

'Just coming's enough, love,' Matthew whispered, hearing the sound of footsteps down the uncarpeted passage behind the door. 'It's you coming what he'll appreciate.'

And when Stanley opened the door, and she saw his thin, suffering face, there was no need for words. To her dismay, tears sprang to his eyes as he opened the door wide for them to pass, and Matthew left them there, staring at each other with a mute and touching obvious affection. By God, but they're really smitten with each other, he thought as he found his own way through into the living-room.

Ada Armstrong was sitting by the inevitable fire, wearing a black cardigan over a navy-blue dress, her face as white as a corpse's, her hands for once idle in her lap. Her lack of surprise at seeing him standing there by the big square table, covered now with a maroon velour cloth, told him that she was in a state of complete and utter shock.

Matthew put his hat on the table. 'Good morning, Mrs Armstrong,' he said. 'I've come to tell you that, if there's owt I can do, tha's only to speak.' He went over to her and touched her gently on her shoulder. 'Tha remembers me? Matthew Bolton, from the mill?'

She nodded, but didn't speak. It was going to be harder than he'd imagined. He put an envelope on the table next to his hat.

'Tha'll be needing this, Mrs Armstrong.' He tapped it with a finger. 'There's folks might think I'm being tactless at a time like this, but I've never been one for keeping me mouth shut when to open it might help. And I don't suppose tha's much put by.'

'Put by?' she said, and the pale lips in the dead-white face lifted just a fraction at the corners.

Matthew moved over to a chair, and lifting the tails of his black overcoat, he sat down. By the gum, but it was hot. What with the sun slanting in through the window and that great fire roaring away up the chimney, already he could feel the beads of perspiration standing out on his

73

forehead. She read his thoughts.

'Three buckets of coal, all left outside 'back door. Folks is very kind.'

'Aye, you find your friends . . .' Matthew nodded. 'And I'm going to tell that lad of yours to come to me for owt you might need . . .'

She looked him straight in the eye, then glanced at the envelope on the table. 'I'll not insult you by refusing, Mr Bolton. You're a good man, but our Stanley will see to things. He's finished all his exams so he'll be stopping off school till after the . . . the funeral.' She tilted her head bravely. 'He might only be a lad, but he's doing what has to be done.'

'This is Dorothy, Mum.'

Stanley came into the room with Dorothy following, and led her over to his mother's chair. 'She's come to see if there's anything she can do.'

'Like running errands, Mrs Armstrong,' Dorothy said, the words she had been rehearsing deserting her completely. 'There must be food you need . . . and I'll know better what to get than Stanley. Or writing letters for you . . .' She faltered. Gosh, that was a silly thing to say. Now this little woman who was staring steadily into that enor- r.ous fire would think *she* thought that she couldn't write. 'Or ironing,' she added desperately, causing Matthew, even in spite of the circumstances, to raise an eyebrow in surprise, as never, to his knowledge, had he seen his younger daughter wielding an iron.

Ada Armstrong nodded, still without looking at Dorothy. She didn't want to look at her, if the truth were known. This was a young girl, not much older than her Ruby had been, a pretty girl with a soft and tender voice, and hair as fair as Ruby's had been dark, curling sweetly round her bonny face.

And she was alive.

And Ruby was dead. . . .

'We have a good neighbour,' Stanley said quickly, step-

74

ping in for his mother. 'She's out doing a bit of shopping now. She says she'll take over me mother's commitments till . . . till . . .' He stopped talking and stared at the floor.

'There's to be a post-mortem. At two o'clock this afternoon,' Ada said then, speaking directly to Matthew. 'He's going down . . . I wanted them to bring her home, but it's not . . . it's just not possible.'

'They'll get him, Mrs Armstrong,' Matthew said. 'They're clever, the police are. They'll leave no stone unturned. Aye . . . Aye,' he said again, standing up and reaching for his hat.

'That won't bring our Ruby back though, will it?' She was rocking the chair gently, backwards and forwards, her face as expressionless as the poker resting in its stand in the hearth.

Again Matthew pressed her shoulder, then he turned to Dorothy. 'I'll be waiting in the car,' he said, and walked out of the room, down the brown-painted passage and out into the street, conscious of twitching curtains as Philips scrambled out and held the door open for him to climb inside. He was conscious of a dismaying sense of anticlimax. He'd said it all wrong. Whatever he'd come to say, he'd said it all wrong. It was all very well feeling sorry from a distance, *sincerely* feeling sorry and wanting to help. But it wasn't brought home to you that what had happened had happened to real people; could have happened to Dorothy. Or Margaret. Damn it, it could have been Phyllis sitting there in a chair having to listen to what was practically a stranger mouthing stupid offers of help. He should have sent the money round from the mill with a messenger . . . and it weren't enough, nowhere near enough. The way she'd looked when he'd said that bit about having a bit put by. Phyllis was right in some ways. There was a big gap, a bloody big gap, and nowt could bridge it. Matthew sat there, brooding into the top of his hat which he'd laid across his knees.

'I'll come again if I may, Mrs Armstrong,' Dorothy was

saying. 'May I come again?'

Ada nodded. 'If you want to, lass. Our Stanley'll be glad to see you.'

'Even if I couldn't care less' her expression said, and overcoming with difficulty a sudden urge to bend and kiss the pale cheek, Dorothy turned away and, choking back tears, walked out of the room.

Behind the front door Stanley put his arms round her. 'I'll not forget you coming,' he whispered. 'It's not that she doesn't like you; it's just that . . .'

'I'm not Ruby,' Dorothy finished for him. Then, as her heart seemed to be physically swelling with emotion inside her, she looked up and gently touched his hair. 'I love you,' she said. 'If it helps to know that, I love you, Stanley.'

Then she was outside in the street, running round the car to get in beside her father, the tears streaming down her cheeks.

The car broke down two streets away from the mill, the engine dying with a splutter as Philips changed into bottom gear. So leaving it standing black and square at the side of the road, they walked the rest of the way, three abreast, Matthew muttering that he'd give that garage what for when he telephoned. 'You can't trust nobody to do a proper job these days,' he said, then turned to Philips. 'It might be better if you went there, now, in person. If I get through it'll only be that bit of a lad in the office. Come back and tell me what they say, and tell them I want that car on the road by this afternoon. And don't take no for an answer,' he shouted as Philips touched the neb of his cap and crossed over the street.

'From the looks of that sky it's going to rain,' he said. 'Shines before seven, rain by eleven. It never fails.'

He glanced sideways at his daughter. Her eyes and the tip of her nose were red, but she seemed to have regained some of her composure. He said impulsively, wanting to comfort, 'He seems a nice lad, that Stanley. I'll talk it out with your mother, chuck . . . we . . . we've been playing it all wrong it seems to me. From now on he can come to the house whenever he wants to. I don't want you hanging about in the park on your own waiting for him, and besides, things is different from when I was a lad. Then, if a young man came to call, it meant but one thing, that wedding bells were in the offing. There were no such thing as having a member of the opposite sex as a *friend*.' He looked at her hopefully, but she said nothing. 'Aye, we've got to move with the times.'

'Mother will never see it that way.' Dorothy's tone was bitter. 'And it had to take his sister's murder before *you* could feel that way.' She knew she was being more than unfair, but she couldn't help it. It was a dramatic statement, and high drama seemed to be the order of the day.

Gerald Tomlin came to the door of the office to greet them. *Shining* with importance, Dorothy told herself.

He fingered his tie as he spoke. 'They've only just left – the police that is, Mr Bolton. I told them you'd be back within the hour, but they couldn't wait.' He raised a hand and smoothed back his already smooth hair. 'They've got a chappie over, a detective sergeant, and he says they're going to start a door-to-door enquiry, checking on every single man in the town. Wanting to know his whereabouts on the night in question.'

Matthew was already shrugging himself out of his overcoat. 'Good. That shows they mean business then. I reckon they'll have him within the week.' Then he sat down at his desk and pulled a sheaf of papers towards him, his mind on the busy day ahead. 'That rain? Aye, I thought as much; tha'll have to get used to the sun being a bit shy up here, Gerald, it doesn't hang about for long.' He read the first letter on top of the pile. 'Seen this one, Gerald? Is this all they can say in answer to the stinker we sent them last week?' He pinched the bridge of his nose between thumb and forefinger. 'Bless my soul, we've got to get you home some way, love. I promised your mother I'd send you back with Philips.'

Dorothy walked over to the window, and watched the rain as it bounced up from the greasy cobbles. She could hear the noise of the looms from the weaving sheds. A sort of muffled banging and clattering. Tolerable at that distance, but to the weavers standing at their looms? A hissing jet of steam came from the side of one of the tall chimneys. At twelve o'clock the loud hoarse hooter would go, and the mill workers would stream out, going home for their dinner, the girl weavers arm in arm, the cotton fluff thick in their hair and on their clothes, and the men walking quickly, avoiding the little groups of men standing idle on the street corners. To have a job was to set a man apart. Stanley had said that. She wrote her initial on the dirty window pane. How filthy everything was, filthy and noisy, the grime was in the very air. No wonder the women, at the first sign of sunshine, had feverishly tried to clean the outside of their houses. No wonder Ruby Armstrong had deceived her mother to meet a man who had perhaps told her that he loved her, promised her he would take her away from all this . . . She'd never had a holiday, Stanley had said. Never, as Dorothy did once a year, in the July wakes week, travelled first class down to Eastbourne and walked across the springy turf of Beachy Head, feeling the wind whipping the colour into her cheeks as she stared down at the sea pounding the rocks far below. And now, at sixteen, Ruby was dead . . . Dorothy crossed out her initial with a fierce and steady cross, the unfairness, the bitter injustice of it choking her throat again with tears.

'It's only a cloudburst,' she said without turning round. 'There's a patch of blue in the sky over there. I'll wait a while, then walk.' She bent her head, unconscious of her father's pitying glance, and the way he shook his head at Gerald Tomlin. 'I'd go straight to school if I'd thought to put my uniform on, but I'd rather wait till Monday really before I go back. They . . . the girls in my form will be

78

talking about it, and asking me things, and I couldn't bear it. I wouldn't know what to say.'

'I'll run her home, Mr Bolton.'

Gerald was behind her, his hand on her shoulder; she could smell the lavender tang of the brilliantine on his hair. 'I can be back in half an hour,' he said.

There wouldn't have been any point in arguing, Dorothy told herself, as she lowered herself into the passenger seat of the red sports car, keeping a tight hold on her skirt. It would have been impossible to explain that she would have liked nothing better than to have walked all the way home alone in the rain. Feeling it beating down on her head, soaking through her blazer, and ruining her new patent-leather shoes. The last thing in the world she wanted was Gerald Tomlin's company; being shut in like this with him, in close and intimate proximity was making her flesh crawl. I must be *allergic* to him, she thought hysterically.

No, if she'd refused, her father would have thought she was mad, as well as rude, and Gerald, sitting beside her, hands resting lightly on the steering wheel, would have interpreted it as another snub. Before starting the car he had lit a cigarette, holding it lightly between his fingers. Without asking her did she mind, as Stanley would have done.

And Mother thinks he's perfect, she thought childishly.

There was one thing you had to admit, and that was his expertise in driving his car. Even with the cigarette in his hand he drove swiftly and smoothly, almost as if the car was an extension of himself. Already the rain was slackening off; umbrellas were being lowered, headscarves untied, and women on their way back from the shops were telling each other that they never knew what to wear these days, what with the weather being the way it was.

'See, the rain's stopped. I could have walked after all,' Dorothy said, and was slightly ashamed at the reproachful look Gerald gave her.

'*Be honest now, you don't give him a chance,*' she told herself silently, then felt even more ashamed as a woman holding a small child by the hand stepped off the pavement without looking. Jamming on the brakes, Gerald put out his left arm in an instinctive gesture of protection to prevent her from being thrown forward against the windscreen.

'You have to be prepared for that,' he told her. 'Sorry if it startled you, love.'

The unexpected endearment, coupled with his genuine concern for her made her feel more ashamed than ever, and his next words made her actually squirm in the low seat with embarrassment.

'You and me seem to have got off on the wrong foot somehow, Dorothy. I wish there was something I could do about it.' Stopping to allow a small group of women board a tram, he turned to her and smiled. 'Am I such a terrible fellow?'

There was nothing she could say to that, and when, turning off the main road, he stopped the car, pulling into the kerb and switching off the engine, she found she could not meet his eyes.

'Perhaps it's time we had a little talk,' he said, winding down the window and throwing the cigarette stub into the road. He put a hand lightly over her own. 'Maybe this is the wrong time . . .' He squeezed her hand gently. 'It must have been simply ghastly for you this morning. It was a very brave thing to do, going to see Stanley and his mother.' Another pat on the hand. 'Have the police come up with anything fresh? They seem to be baffled by the total absence of clues.'

'There's to be a post-mortem this afternoon,' she said in a low voice.

Letting go of her hand he reached for another cigarette. 'Ah, well, I suppose that was inevitable.' He busied himself with his lighter. 'Did you know the . . . the dead girl personally, Dorothy? What I mean is, would you have said she was the confiding type? Likely to tell her brother anything that might help the police?'

She shook her head. 'I can't remember ever having *spoken* to her, and no, that's the awful thing, she must have kept her meetings with whoever did this dreadful thing quite private.'

He blew out a stream of smoke, then wafted it away from her face, apologizing. 'But you know the brother *very* well?'

There was a teasing quality in his voice now, and she blushed. 'Margaret must have told you.'

'Margaret tells me everything. That's how it should be.' He smiled at her. 'I love your sister very much, you know that, don't you? And I intend to love and cherish her for ever. You know that too, don't you?'

Dorothy nodded, wishing that he would start the car again and drive on.

'And because I feel that way, I find the fact that her little sister doesn't like me, *very* hard to bear.'

'But I don't . . .'

'I know what you're thinking. You're surprised that a bloke like me who comes from south of the Wash should be so outspoken. You think that you and your fellow Lancastrians have the monopoly in calling a spade a spade. That I, because of my public school background, should be all stiff upper lip. But you could be wrong, Dorothy Bolton, with your bright gold hair, and those blue eyes that look at me and find me wanting.'

She stretched out her legs and studied her shoes. He had the most beautiful voice, she would say that for him, and perhaps, maybe she hadn't really been fair to him? But he was holding her hand again, and she wished he would take it away. There were little tufts of ginger hair sprouting from between the knuckles, and something about his touch that repelled her. How *could* Margaret find him so fascinating? She forced herself to meet his eyes, and was immediately thrown into confusion by the wealth of sadness she saw reflected there.

This man, this red-haired stranger who had come into their lives, was unsure of himself. He was pleading with her to like him, as if it mattered a great deal, as if he couldn't bear her rejection of him. She began to pleat her skirt with her free hand.

'Has it ever occurred to you that I am not the over-confident type you obviously think I am, Dorothy? That coming up here and finding Margaret, and being accepted into your family gives me such happiness that I am afraid? Yes. Afraid, positively scared.' Dorothy smoothed out the pleats she had made, then started again.

'My father was a colonel in the Indian Army, and when I was a small child, I was left in the care of an aunt and uncle who gave me everything but love. Then, as soon as I was old enough, I was sent away to school, and because my aunt was by then an invalid – nerves mostly, which didn't help – I spent the shorter hols in the charge of school matrons.' His eyes, surely the palest of blue she had ever seen, twinkled at her. 'Why do all school matrons have busts like upholstered shelves and fierce moustaches, I wonder?' He closed his eyes for a moment, then went on: 'When my parents were killed I was told of their deaths so casually that the person who told me might have been passing the time of day. And from then on it was nothing but a lonely determination to pass my accountancy exams; a constant fight against the temptation to give it all up and get a job which would help me to live at a decent standard.' He puffed vigorously at the cigarette. 'I don't want to bore you with a description of what the past ten years have been like, but all I can say is that coming up here and falling in love with Margaret, and being accepted as part of your family has shown me that my own personal barometer is rising at last.' He touched the tip of her nose lightly with his finger.

'And the only fly in the ointment is me?' Dorothy whispered, but she was half smiling, and did not cringe away as he leaned forward and kissed her cheek.

'You *frightened* me,' he said, 'with your way of looking at me with those lovely eyes narrowed into suspicious slits, as if you were determined to think the worst of me. And I've been a bit of a bounder in my time, I admit. Girls and booze you know, but nothing serious . . .'

He knows that I saw him flirting in the mill yard, Dorothy thought, and he's trying to tell me that all that's past. . . .

'But as soon as I fell in love with Margaret and she with me, the slate was wiped clean,' he was saying now. 'So do you think we could start again, Dorothy, so soon to be my sister? From this very moment?'

Then, without waiting for a reply he switched on the engine and pulled swiftly and smoothly away from the kerb.

And then they were driving up the road which ran at the side of the park, and he was putting his foot down hard on the accelerator.

And for some unknown unearthly reason Dorothy found that she was thinking about her much loved Grandfather Bolton, with his waxed moustache and the wrapped sweet in his top pocket waiting there for her childish fingers to find. At his death she had been desolate, but her father had taken her on his knee, big as she was.

'Grandpa hasn't gone, lovey,' he'd said. 'The ones we love never die, not really. The things they've said come back to us, at the right times, to comfort us, and to guide us . . . tha'll see.'

And what Grandpa Bolton was saying was as clear as if he'd been there beside her. He was twiddling with the pointed ends of his glorious moustache and smiling.

'A man what touts for sympathy never deserves it,' she remembered him saying. 'It's the chap what says nowt that we come to admire.'

Now when and where had the old man said that, and why should she remember it just at this moment? Of one thing she was quite sure. Gerald Tomlin wouldn't have been Grandpa Bolton's cup of tea either.

Seven

Dorothy was no more surprised to find that her Auntie
Ethel had called round than her mother had been when the
door-bell rang before ten o'clock that morning. What was
in the papers was far too interesting to discuss over the
telephone. And a murder almost in the family so to speak!
The sister of the boy her niece Dorothy was supposed to be
so friendly with! Well, that would be one in the eye, however kindly meant of course, for her sister who had always
got the biggest plums since they were little girls. There'd
been no doing with her since Margaret had got herself
engaged. Ethel could just see her at the wedding. Perfectly
dressed as usual, Phyllis always seemed to get the right
thing, whereas she, Ethel, no matter how much she paid,
never seemed to add up all of a piece somehow. She wasn't
jealous, of course she wasn't, but it wouldn't do Phyllis any
harm to be taken down a peg or two, and she'd said as much
to Raymond that morning after Gerald had left the house,
driving his car out of the drive as if he were on his way to his
own funeral, and late at that.

'But there's nothing serious between Dorothy and that
boy,' Raymond had said, looking at her over the top of his
spectacles. 'They're still at school, the both of them. It's
only a boy and girl friendship, and what can you expect
when they're still at school at their age?'

'Ha, ha,' Ethel had said, signifying that she knew a lot
more than she was prepared to say, and regretting from the
bottom of her heart that she didn't.

No, Dorothy wasn't in the least surprised to see her Auntie Ethel sitting there, with the inevitable hat skewered to her greying hair. But she was surprised to see her cousin Beryl sitting dead centre of the big chintz-covered chesterfield, the red blazer and skirt of the private school at the bottom of West Road doing less than nothing for her sallow complexion.

'Seems like you're both playing truant this morning,' Ethel said, munching on a Marie biscuit. 'Beryl's got a bad period, haven't you, love? What she goes through every month is nobody's business, though it was just the same with me at her age. Do you rememer, Phyllis? Worse than labour pains my cramps were.'

Dorothy saw her mother flinch, and accepting a cup of coffee gratefully, wondered, not for the first time, how two sisters could have had the same mother and father, been brought up in the same house, and yet turn out so entirely different? Periods at Appleroyd were things to be endured, never spoken of, a feminine nuisance, along with childbirth, and what her mother called *that* side of marriage.

'I well remember the agonies I went through on the day I was confirmed,' Auntie Ethel was saying. 'Mother had had our white dresses made at Madge Gardener's little place round the back of the Emporium, do you remember? Nice little woman who skenned like a basket of whelks, never knew which eye to talk to. Anyway, what was I saying? Oh yes. There I was in that white dress, sure that when I walked up the aisle there'd be a patch . . .'

Phyllis could take no more. She actually put up a hand as if to stop the traffic, and turned to Dorothy. 'That sounded like Gerald's car turning round in the drive, dear? What happened to Philips? I wanted him to get the blind down from the attic for the front door. We don't want the new paint coming up in blisters.'

Dorothy sat down next to Beryl and smiled at her. 'The car broke down,' she explained, 'and Father sent Philips to the garage to see if they could send someone out to it straight away. We weren't far from the mill, so we walked, then Gerald offered to bring me home.'

'Lovely manners,' Ethel said, reaching for another biscuit. 'A public school gives a boy something you can't get anywhere else. Raymond says it's because they train them to be leaders. Do you know that, even though he's been staying with us all this time, he still stands up when I go out of the room? And he won't touch a thing on his plate till I've picked my spoon up – or my fork. Lovely.'

Then, as if suddenly remembering what she'd come for, she turned to Dorothy. 'I hope it wasn't too harrowing for you this morning, love, going down Inkerman Street. Your mother told me how you felt you had to go, and I will say this for you, Dorothy, you've always stuck by your friends, no matter what they've done.'

Dorothy bowed her head. *Oh, God, it was awful. They were all sitting there like vultures, waiting to pounce. Waiting for her to tell them something that the papers hadn't managed to get hold of. Even her mother, sitting there with her knees pressed close together, hoping she wouldn't say too much, but fascinated just the same. And Auntie Ethel with her round eyes starting from her head like chapel hat pegs, as Grandpa Bolton would have said . . . Why did he keep coming into her mind. Why?*

'Well?' the three pairs of eyes queried.

'I don't suppose you stayed more than a minute,' Phyllis said, giving her the cue.

Dorothy shook her head. 'There's to be a post-mortem this afternoon,' she told them reluctantly. 'At two o'clock.'

Ethel nodded with satisfaction. 'To see if she was interfered with; there's some men should have it chopped off and that's a fact.'

Phyllis's thick eyelids lowered themselves like defensive shutters. 'Why don't you and Beryl go upstairs, dear? You can show her the drawings Margaret made for the head-dresses, and see what she thinks.' She drew a circle in the air with her forefinger. 'It's a round wreath, Ethel. Tiny rosebuds, we thought, and I've booked the three girls in for

86

early appointments at Pierre's. You wouldn't consider having Beryl's hair permed? Say, just the ends?'

Firmly Ethel shook her head. 'It takes the nature out,' she said, 'all that baking. It stands to reason.'

Phyllis sighed. 'Ah well. I'm having mine done the day before of course. I'll be far too busy to go into town on *the* morning. If I pin it well and keep my net on it should be quite all right.'

'Your mother only sent us upstairs so that you wouldn't say anything else about the murder,' Beryl said, sitting down gingerly on the edge of Dorothy's bed. 'I think it's awful the way everybody's going on about it. I'm not going to ask you anything about it, so don't think I am. I saw Stanley Armstrong the other day when I was coming out of school. He was running down West Road, and he looked awful.'

'I didn't know you knew him?'

'I've seen you together lots of times, coming out of the side park gates. But you never saw me.' Her glance was sly, and Dorothy turned away to hide the hated blush.

'Gosh, I do wish I'd been born a boy,' Beryl went on. 'It was awful in the night. I was rolling about in bed with pain. Mother says she'd take me to a specialist in Manchester if she wasn't sure I'd grow out of it. I can never be in the netball team or anything because if it comes on the day I'd be there sitting on a deck-chair in the cloakroom with a hot-water bottle on my stomach and Miss Haydock giving me hot water with Indian brandy in it.'

'Is that what you have to do when you're ill? Sit on a deck-chair in the cloakroom?'

'There's nowhere else.' Beryl rubbed hard at her stomach. 'Yes, I do wish I'd been a boy.'

Dorothy sat down on the padded stool at her dressing-table, and privately agreed that life would have been easier for Cousin Beryl if she had been a boy. An only child, she would, if she'd been a he, have gone straight into her

87

father's timber business, needing neither Matriculation nor Higher School Certificate, nor indeed any of the social graces Auntie Ethel seemed determined to drum into Beryl. Music lessons, elocution, extra coaching in French, and dresses made by Ethel's own dressmaker, a Miss Randle, whose idea of chic was to have enough material left over for a matching belt and a push-back beret style hat. She looked in the mirror and saw her cousin's reflection. She really did look rotten. The round face had a greenish tinge to it, and as she drooped forward, her greasy hair fell over her face, not quite concealing two angry red spots on her chin.

'What sort of a mood was Gerald in when he brought you home just now?' she asked unexpectedly.

Dorothy pulled a face at herself in the mirror. 'Oh, oozing charm as usual. He told me his life story, wanting me to feel sorry for him for some reason. Why do you ask?'

Beryl jerked her head upwards, presenting a suffering face to the ceiling. 'Because he was really snotty at breakfast, that's why. I thought perhaps he and Margaret had had a lovers' tiff. They went to the pictures last night, didn't they?'

'How did you know that?'

'Because I asked him where he was going, that's why. Usually he just says "out" when I ask him. Mother says I shouldn't ask him so many questions, but I worked it out when he first came to stay with us that it would be the only way of getting him to talk to me. He ignores me. I could be a stick of furniture for all he knows or cares, he certainly doesn't use his charm on me. That's because I'm not pretty like you, and I'm not, so you don't need to say I am. Oh, I do wish I'd been a boy, 'cos looks wouldn't have mattered then. I mean to say, look at your Stanley. Nobody could say he's good-looking, now could they? He's too thin for one thing, and pale. Not like Gerald. He's got lovely colour, hasn't he? Do you know who I think he'd be the spit image of if he had dark hair? Ronald Colman. His voice is exactly the same . . . Gosh, fancy being married to someone like that! Your Margaret doesn't know how lucky she is.'

What was it Margaret had said? Dorothy shook her head sadly as she remembered: '*Beryl stares at him when he's eating. And follows him about asking him personal questions. If we weren't getting married soon Gerald says he'd have to find somewhere else to stay. She's driving him bonkers.*'

Oh poor Cousin Beryl. It had been the same for as long as Dorothy could remember. Always in love with someone; for ever nursing an unrequited passion for the most unlikely people. The biology mistress. Taking little posies of flowers to school and leaving them with anonymous little notes on her desk. That tall boy in the choir, the golden-haired one who snuffed out the candles before the sermon with the air of knowing how beautiful he looked doing it. Before his voice had broken Beryl had gone to every service on Sundays, sitting where she could feast her eyes on him, and once drawing his profile in the flyleaf of her hymn book. Once, a long time ago, she had put her arm round Dorothy's waist and said, '*Let's be best friends for ever, you and me, and tell each other everything, shall we?*'

With a feeling akin to shame Dorothy remembered the way she had stiffened and moved away, muttering that she didn't want to be best friends with anyone, that best friends weren't her line at all. She looked at the bowed figure, the drooping head, and with a flash of intuition realized that this was the way it would always be for Beryl. Always swooning with love for someone unattainable. Perhaps deliberately unattainable . . . The issues were too complex for her to unravel at the moment; her mind was still reeling with the shock of seeing Stanley and his mother trapped in their inconsolable grief. In more normal times she would have discussed it with Stanley in the way they sometimes would spend hours discussing other people's idiosyncrasies.

'*You'd think there was only thee and me normal,*' he had said once after they had spent a satisfactory half-hour analysing her mother's motivations. Yes, Stanley would have had a very satisfactory theory about Beryl. . . .

And now she had fixed on Gerald. Driving him mad with questions; watching him, *prying*, just so he would have to talk to her.

'He hasn't gone out in the evenings as much lately,' Beryl was saying gloomily. 'Before he got engaged to Margaret he used to go out almost every night in his car.' She fingered one of the spots on her chin sadly. 'When I asked him where he was going, he laughed and said he just liked driving alone. Fast, in the dark all on his own. Out as far as the moors. It made me think of Heathcliff wandering alone over the moors looking for someone to love.'

'Heathcliff?' Dorothy's reaction was more disparaging than she had intended it to be. 'I can't think of anyone less like Heathcliff than Gerald Tomlin. For one thing Heathcliff didn't drive over the moors in a red MG sports car. He *strode*.'

'I'm glad he's found happiness at last. He's got such a lovely accent.'

'He talks like an ha'penny book,' Dorothy said, getting up from the stool. 'Let's have a look at the sketches, shall we? I've had just about enough of Gerald for one morning.'

'I simply love weddings, don't you?' Beryl trailed along the landing, walking carefully. 'Gosh, wouldn't it be awful if Margaret had her you know what on her wedding day? Won't it be beady if they have a baby straight away?'

Eight

'You can talk about inquests and post mortems till the cows come home,' Ada Armstrong said, her face set in stubborn lines of disbelief. 'But if our Ruby had been expecting I'd have known.' She glanced at Stanley, then away and at Mrs Crawley. 'Tha's only a lad and not supposed to know about such things, but you can't live in a house like this with the only privacy being if tha goes out and bolts theself in the outside lavatory. And anyway, our Ruby weren't that sort of girl. If she'd thought she was like that and her not wed she'd have been half out of her mind. She couldn't have kept a thing like that from me.'

Mrs Crawley's face, beneath the inevitable halo of day-time curlers, was soft with compassion. No gleam of fascinated interest, Stanley noted, no shocked surprise even, certainly no wait-till-I-tell-the-neighbours attitude. Just honest-to-goodness sympathy, and a desire to help.

'They said she was almost three months gone,' Stanley said, turning to Nellie Crawley. 'So if it was the same man who killed her — and they're sure it must have been now there's a motive, so to speak — that would mean she was meeting him around Christmas time.' He turned back to his mother. 'Mum, we've got to *think*. What did she do about Christmas time? Did she go to any parties? I know some of the girls from the mill had parties . . .'

'She weren't like that,' Ada said, shaking her head as if she would shake the words away. 'I would stake my life that Ruby weren't like that. She was a good girl . . . a good girl.'

'It's the good ones what get caught,' Mrs Crawley said. 'The poor little sod. She must have been well nigh out of her mind, keeping that to herself.' She shook a finger at Ada. 'And it's not the worst sin now, Mrs Armstrong, not by a long chalk. I've always thought that. There's bloody-mindedness, and coldness, and meanness, and lust. Aye, lust, Mrs Armstrong. And I'll swear by our Holy Mother that your Ruby weren't guilty of none of them.' She jerked her head in the direction of the scullery and winked at Stanley. 'Put the kettle on, there's a good lad, and you sit you down, Mrs Armstrong. You've had more than you can take, and that's a bloody fact.'

Ada looked at her piteously. 'How could I not know? What's been happening in this house, for the love of God? Me only daughter meeting some man on the sly all these past weeks, and having his baby, and I didn't suspect? What sort of a mother have I been? Why couldn't I see there was something sadly wrong with her?' She looked for a confirmation that could not be given. 'How long did she think she could keep it from me? I'd have tried to understand. Even if she wouldn't tell me who it was – and he was a married man, I'm more convinced of it than ever now – I would have stood by her.'

'Of course you would, love.' Mrs Crawley was guiding her gently towards the rocking chair. 'You're not the sort of mother to throw her daughter out on the streets because she makes a slip. You'd have looked after her and then you'd have brought up the baby yourself while she went back to work.' The curlers glistened in a sudden shaft of sunlight as she got carried away. 'You'd have put him in yon basket where them shirts are, you would, and if any of the neighbours 'ad said anything, you'd have spit in their eye.' She patted Ada's arm. 'And I'd have spit in t'other one for you, love, that I would.'

'It was an older man,' Ada said, picking up her pressing cloth from the table and twisting it round and round in her hands as she talked. 'I've thought so all along, and I'm saying it again. Ruby went out with Eddie next door for a good twelve-month, and I'll swear there was nothing going on. She had her head screwed on all right, and she'd have known how to handle Eddie Marsden if he'd started anything.' The piece of fent tore down the middle and she flung it from her. 'So it must have been an older man, one with a smooth tongue, a *persuasive* sort of man who could undo in one minute all that I've been telling her since she grew up. "Never sell yourself cheap" I used to tell her. "If a man wants to marry you enough, he'll wait."'

'Not like my bugger,' Mrs Crawley said, lowering her voice in the vain hope that Stanley out in the scullery wouldn't hear. 'I were four-month gone when we got wed, then just two weeks to the day after the wedding I lost it. And that were it.' She gave her cackle of a laugh. 'Maybe it were all that jumping down steps and sitting in a tin bath swiggin' gin what did it. Any road I never had another chance.' She winked at Ada. 'And it weren't for t'want of trying, not in them early days it weren't.'

It was no use deciding not to listen. Not a bit of use closing the scullery door that was never closed anyway. Mrs Crawley's voice carried like a clarion call. She was talking about the funeral now.

'How much did you have on 'er, love?'

'Nothing. Harry didn't believe in insurance.'

'Well, I've never heard nowt like that before. I've had twopence on me husband and threepence on me mother-in-law for years. If she doesn't die quick I'll have bought all t'bloody cemetery.'

Stanley waited for the kettle to come to the boil. They seemed to have forgotten that he was there . . . He could feel a sickening sensation churning away in his bowels. He kicked absent-mindedly at the frayed piece of coconut-matting laid over the flagged floor.

Not Ruby. Not his sister, the quiet, gentle, dark-haired

girl who had had to go in the mill so that he, Stanley, could study and swot to his heart's content in a room of his own. Had her pride in his scholastic achievements been more mixed with envy than he had guessed? Had she sought comfort in the arms of some unknown man because the conditions at home had become intolerable to her? Had she resented more bitterly than he could hope to have guessed the fact that she had had to work in some weaving shed whilst he stayed on at school? Had she given herself – he used the phrase without a trace of self-consciousness – to this man with a silver tongue who had promised her an escape and ended up with his hands round her throat, squeezing the life out of her?

The sick feeling in his stomach was growing worse. He opened the back door and took a few deep breaths, then he turned off the gas underneath the kettle, closed the back door softly behind him and went outside. Down the three stone steps, past the meat safe, down the sloping backyard with the low soot-blackened walls separating it from its neighbours, out to the lavatory, where he bolted himself inside.

It was what Mrs Crawley had said. Meant kindly but bringing home to him as nothing else had that Ruby was dead. DEAD. 'How much did you have on her, love?' Oh, God, the man from the Prudential knocking at the door on Friday nights, early, before the tea-things were cleared away in the street, catching folks before they went out to spend their wages if they'd been lucky enough to have a week's work behind them. Twopence on our Edie, threepence on me dad. No wonder his father had thought the whole system barbaric . . . and yet. . . .

Now they would have to plan the funeral, or at least *he* would have to plan the funeral. There'd be people they hardly knew in shiny black, and his mother leaning on his arm, with the neighbours in the street watching with compassion. With compassion, aye, but watching just the same.

94

Shut away in the tiny enclosed space, he stared round him at the white-washed walls, the squares of newspaper hanging by a string from a nail, shut away, he scuffed with his feet the tattered rag rug on the flagged floor. Over the outside wall, out in the back he could hear the children from the house three doors up shouting to each other as they came home from school. Old Mrs Preston was calling her cat in, banging on a tin plate, crying its name. The man next door, out of work now for eighteen months, pulled the lavatory chain and shuffled his way back into the house, and streets away the rag-and-bone man called out his unintelligible cry. Life was going on, would go on just the same after Ruby was forgotten. He, Stanley Armstrong, would get up in the mornings and go to work, if he'd been lucky enough to find a job. His mother would wash more shirts, Dorothy would leave school and start as a typist in her father's office, and in a few years' time she would marry a young fellow who was a director in his father's firm. They'd have the reception at The Pied Bull over on the edge of the moors, and their photographs would be in the weekly paper, laughing into each other's eyes, with a description of the bridesmaids' dresses underneath. And all this would be a million years away.

And if you'd asked him, he couldn't have told you why he suddenly felt an aching, terrible despair, so that the sobs tore at his throat with a rasping noise that made him stuff his fist into his mouth. He knew that he was crying for his sister, for what seemed to be the death, too, of all his hopes, but there was more. There was something else his tormented brain was weeping for. His ideals, his unexpressed emotions about love and tenderness. And lust. Mrs Crawley had been right to use that word. He, Stanley Armstrong, had lusted after Dorothy Bolton. He'd dreamed of her, but in his dreams his love for her had been no more than a stroking of her yellow hair, a holding her close, a kissing of her eyelids.

The tears ran down over his hand and he groaned aloud.

But that wasn't love. Not the reality of love. Love was Mrs Crawley sitting in a tin bath and drinking gin, and love was Ruby lying on the grass with the weight of some unknown man above her. And love was Ruby dead with a leaf caught up in her hair.

Mrs Crawley's voice could be heard calling out from the open back door.

'Are you all right, love? Your mum wants to know. Are you all right out there?'

But he made he reply, just stayed there with the agony of disillusionment growing inside him as if it were a living thing.

Nine

'Where was he ringing from, dear? I shouldn't think Mrs Armstrong is on the telephone, is she?'

Phyllis's voice breathed a tolerance she was obviously far from feeling. It had been a most trying day again, with Dorothy mooning round the house with a cold that didn't seem all that much in evidence, and Mrs Wilkinson going on and on asking questions.

'My heart grieves for that poor dead girl and her family, but I have never met any of them, so I can't tell you *anything*, Mrs Wilkinson,' she had said. 'Our only connection is in that she worked in the weaving shed, and that Dorothy has been walking home from school with her brother.'

'And that hardly makes us *relatives*,' she'd added under her breath.

Even Gerald had rung and tried to wriggle out of taking Margaret to the Police Ball that night. She'd heard only one side of the conversation of course, but she could tell that Margaret had been quite put out about it. And quite rightly when they'd had the tickets for weeks. Phyllis was reduced to playing patience, a ploy she always used when under stress, just as some women scrubbed floors or others went out and bought themselves a new hat. She laid a black jack over a red queen.

The last straw had been when Ethel called round and asked if she would be going to the funeral.

'As a token of respect merely,' she'd added quickly, seeing the look on her sister's face. 'On account of the girl

97

working for Matthew, and with Dorothy being her brother's little friend.'

And now Dorothy was refusing to answer what was surely a perfectly straightforward question. Phyllis repeated it: 'Where was Stanley ringing from, dear? I don't suppose anyone in Inkerman Street is on the telephone, are they?'

Her younger daughter came and drooped in the doorway, her face pale, and her blue eyes shadowed as if she hadn't slept for a week.

'No, Mother, they use tom-toms to communicate with each other down that end of the town,' she said. Then as if she knew she had gone too far she went on: 'Stanley was ringing me from a house at the top end of the street. The man living there is a Trade Union Secretary, and in cases of emergency he lets the neighbours pay to use his telephone. He's a kind man apparently. Stanley says he even went out of his own living-room so that he could be private.' She hesitated for a moment, then sighed. 'Ruby was going to have a baby.'

Phyllis's small face seemed to set itself neatly into lines of smug satisfaction. She tapped with the edge of a playing card on the polished table.

'There you are, then. I'm not surprised, not in the least.'

'Stanley and his mother were *very* surprised,' Dorothy said quietly.

Phyllis turned up an ace and laid it down in triumph. 'Well, of course they would be. A mother is always the last person to believe that sort of thing of her own daughter, not that she wouldn't have stood by her, I'm quite sure she would. But at least it gives the police more to work on.' She frowned at the eight of spades.

'What do you mean by that, Mother?'

'Well, now the police know the kind of girl she was, they will know the kind of man to look for.' She shuffled the cards together in exasperation. 'I knew it wasn't going to come out. Yes, he was probably one of many, and when the girl

98

told him that she was going to say he was the father of her child, he lost his temper and killed her. It won't be the first murder to happen that way, and it won't be the last. Especially if he happened to be a married man. Oh yes, it puts a different complexion on the whole thing now. Dorothy! Where are you going? Must you always walk away when I try to talk to you?'

Dorothy was walking slowly upstairs, wondering vaguely if she was in any way psychic. Or just plain fanciful? Watching her mother's small mouth as she talked, the playing cards held neatly in her well-manicured hands, she had felt again that strange sense of evil, of impending horror. In her own house, the house she had been born in, solid, red-bricked, its dark mahogany furniture gleaming from Mrs Wilkinson's ministrations. Something terrible was going to happen, she knew it. The knowledge of it was a crawling in her scalp, a feeling in her very bones. She stood on the landing, quite still, rubbing the tops of her arms as if she felt a sudden draught.

She could still hear the heartbreak in Stanley's voice when he spoke to her, using the clipped exaggerated emphasis of words as people did when they were unaccustomed to using a telephone.

'Ruby wasn't promiscuous. She was a very reserved, private sort of girl . . . you know?'

'You don't have to be promiscuous to start a baby.' Whispering in the hope that her mother wouldn't be able to hear. 'It must have been someone she thought she was in love with. Someone she *was* in love with, I mean.'

'I agree, but it's shaken my mother up. She feels it must have been all her fault somehow. Her not guessing and everything, then Ruby not wanting to tell her. She wouldn't have been turned out of the house or anything. My mother has strong principles but she's not a hard person. She would have understood and tried to help.'

'Of course she would.'

They had never talked on the telephone before, and there

was an awkward breathing silence between them, the shyness that came down like a barrier at times, made worse by the proximity of others.

'I'd best be going then, Dorothy.'

She had lowered her voice, her glance going towards the sitting-room door, open a fraction, imagining her mother with the pack of playing cards in her hand, the neat head on one side in a listening attitude.

'Will I be seeing you after school next week?'

Stanley coughed, forgetting he was holding the receiver, and she jumped. 'I'm not going back till after the funeral . . . I have a lot of things to sort out in my mind. About Oxford. I may have to get a job, as a clerk, anything. I want to talk to you, but it isn't easy at the moment . . .'

'Is it very awful, love?'

'If I wasn't there to tell her to come to the table, to go to bed, and to get up, I think she would just sit there without moving. Mrs Crawley says it's the shock. The minister's been from the chapel, but he said all the wrong things . . .'

Dorothy started to go into her own room, then changed her mind. She didn't feel like being alone, and Margaret was there next door getting ready for the Police Ball. She would listen. She would tell her that Stanley *couldn't* give up his chance of going to university, not after winning a state scholarship. Against overwhelming odds he'd *won* his right to go. . . .

'Is that you, Dorothy?'

Margaret sounded gay and happy. 'Come in and talk to me, I'm almost ready.'

And as usual Margaret was bewailing the fact that she looked a positive mess whilst looking as pretty as a picture on the lid of a box of chocolates. Dorothy could see it . . . a garlanded swing with Margaret laughing at a blue sky with her pink and blue net skirts billowing round her. She was busily applying vaseline to her eyelids, rubbing it in with the tip of her little finger, then closing her eyes and squinting in the mirror from underneath lowered eyelashes to get the effect. She spoke without turning round, carefully, so as not to disturb the petunia-shaded lipstick on her wide mouth.

'For a minute I thought when the phone rang that it might be Gerald. He didn't want to go to the dance tonight for some reason, but I did what Mother does when she persuades Father into changing his mind . . .' Margaret smeared the vaseline over the top of her lipstick. 'I told him it didn't matter in the least; that I couldn't care less whether we went or not, and he was so taken aback it ended with him persuading *me* to go!' She peered anxiously down the front of her dress. 'You don't think this dress is a wee bit low in front, do you? I'd pin my pearl brooch across it, if I could find it. I've looked in my jewel-case and it's not there.'

Dorothy walked across to the wardrobe. 'The last time you wore it you had it pinned to the neckline of your green and brown dress.' She produced the dress with a flourish. 'There you are! You must have forgotten to take it off when you put the dress away.'

Tongue protruding slightly, Margaret pinned the brooch at the middle point of the sweetheart neckline of her dress. She pouted. 'It's a bit scratchy, but nothing shows, that's the main thing.'

She looked so seriously worried that Dorothy, in spite of her mood of depression, laughed out loud. 'Doesn't Gerald know that you've got bosoms, then?'

Margaret answered her quite literally, unaware as usual that she was being teased. 'Well, of course he does, silly. We *are* engaged, remember. No, it's not that, it's just that he can't bear other men staring at me.'

Dorothy fidgeted round the room, picking up the small gilt clock from the bedside table, holding it to her ear, then putting it down again, picking up the white fur jacket from the bed and holding it to her cheek for a moment. 'Is he very passionate, your Gerald?'

Margaret wasn't offended. At eighteen Dorothy was

bound to be becoming curious about such things. She felt quite matronly as she answered her. 'He's had a past, of course,' she confided with more than a touch of pride. 'One couldn't expect anything else with him being a man of the world and living on his own in London for so long. But he *respects* me.' She patted the brooch with a satisfied hand. 'Mother says it's far better for a bride if the man is experienced when they get married.'

Dorothy dabbed behind her ears with Margaret's scent, a woody perfume she decided she didn't much care for. 'But wrong for the girl to be?'

'Well, of *course*, Dorothy. No man wants shop-soiled goods now, does he?'

Dorothy started to answer. Actually opened her mouth to answer, then closed it again. How can we be sisters? she asked herself, silently and dramatically, searching the ceiling as if looking for the answer. Sisters, flesh of the same flesh, blood of the same blood, brought up together in the same house, of the same environment exactly? How can we be so close when we think so differently? She felt suddenly very, very old; at least twice as old as Margaret, and ten times as wise. Rather wistfully she unfolded a pink chiffon hankie lying on the dressing-table and sniffed the pink powder-puff nestling inside, leaving a smear of rose rachel powder on the tip of her nose.

'I only wish Gerald could find his cuff-links as easily as you found my brooch,' she heard Margaret saying.

Dorothy saw the reflection of her eyes widening in surprise in the mirror. She had been with Margaret to choose the cuff-links as an engagement present for Gerald, and the memory of the time it had taken to decide on a suitable gift was still sharp in her memory. For over half an hour she had stood at the counter of Adamson's, the jewellers in King Edward Street, hopping from one foot to the other with impatience as Mr Adamson himself had spread the counter with a piece of black velvet, laying out tie-pins, wristlet watches and cuff-links in a shining display. Margaret's final choice had been the cuff-links because they were shaped like flattened hearts.

'Symbolic,' Margaret had sighed.

'Most unusual,' Mr Adamson had said, winking slyly at Dorothy.

'But how *could* he have lost them?' she said sharply, then she saw Margaret's face flush with loyalty.

'People do lose things, you know, Dorothy, and Gerald's terribly upset about it. In fact, he made me promise not to tell anyone he'd lost them. They're sure to turn up, he says, so for heaven's sake don't tell Mother, or you can imagine . . .' Her voice tailed off in mid-sentence as the unmistakable sound of Gerald's car was heard in the drive outside.

'He's here!' she cried, and Dorothy thought she looked as if a candle had been lit inside her head, so that her mouth and eyes radiated light. Like a turnip on Hallowe'en night, she thought, not very poetically.

But even she had to admit that they made a beautiful couple as they left for the dance, and whilst Phyllis twittered round Gerald, pressing him to a sherry to 'put them in the right mood for a lovely evening together' she intercepted the look he gave his fiancée as surreptitiously he raised one arm slightly to show her that the cuff-links were safely restored to their rightful place in the starched turn-back cuffs of his dress shirt.

'I could have sworn they were smaller than that,' Dorothy muttered to herself as she stood with her mother and waved them off from the door.

'What did you say, dear?' Phyllis asked.

'Oh, nothing,' Dorothy said. 'Just thinking aloud, that's all.'

'I think I'll go mad and have another sherry,' Phyllis said, with the air of one who felt that she deserved some kind of solace.

Ten

'I can't expect Mrs Crawley to go to the market for me; she's doing far more than enough already, and I've never been one for putting on kindness,' Ada Armstrong said. 'But what she pays for her greengrocery at the new shop down on the bottom doesn't bear thinking about. Mr Crawley's in work of course, so she doesn't have to count her pennies like we do.' She pushed at her hair until it stood up straight away from her forehead as if she'd been startled by a headless ghost. 'No, I can't expect her to go down the market late this afternoon when they're selling some things off cheap, and it wouldn't do for me to be seen out till after the funeral – wouldn't be decent.'

Stanley closed his eyes, sending up a silent prayer that at last his mother was showing what the doctor would have called an *interest*. 'I'll go down if you like, Mum.'

'Life must go on,' the minister from the chapel had said, and he supposed that an interest in cut oranges and bruised tomatoes could be interpreted as a beginning. Besides, the claustrophobic atmosphere of the tiny living-room with its banked-up fire, its steaming clothes and continual coming and going of neighbours with offerings of seed-cakes and batches of soda scones was beginning to get on his nerves. He knew he was being selfish and that his place was by his mother's side, but he wanted to feel the wind on his face, wanted to run and run until his heart pounded in his ears, wanted to see Dorothy and talk to her about his decision to leave school and forego his place at university – wanted to

104

forget, just for a little while, what had happened.

Once or twice, whilst Mrs Crawley talked with his mother, helping to fold the washing brought in from the backyard, he had escaped upstairs to his bedroom, and sitting down at the card-table by the window had opened a book, had even taken his pen and dipped it into the bottle of blue-black ink, putting himself out of reach of Mrs Crawley's darting tongue and the closed-in misery of his mother's face.

Through the net curtains he could see the walled-in backyards of the houses opposite in Balaclava Street, drenched in brilliant sunshine, the tin baths hanging on the walls, the coal-sheds and the outside lavatories — even sometimes a glimpse of their white-washed interiors. One particularly sunny afternoon a woman had appeared from her back door carrying a battered deck-chair, and there, just as if she were setting it up on the sand facing the sea at Blackpool in wakes week, she had positioned it next to the dustbin. Then lying back in it she had lifted her skirt to expose fat white thighs, and closed her eyes. A sleek grey cat had joined her, curling itself up on the flagstones, and after a while the woman had unbuttoned her blouse, turning the revers in so that the top curves of her enormous breasts were revealed, offering herself to the sun like a sacrifice.

He had watched her fascinated and repelled at one and the same time, staring until his eyes ached at the corners, then jerking himself back to reality as he heard footsteps on the stairs and the sound of Mrs Crawley's voice coming through the thin plywood his father had erected to separate the two rooms.

'I'm being honest, Mrs Armstrong, I'm your friend and I wouldn't let you go to your own daughter's funeral looking a sight now, would I? And navy blue's every bit as respectable as black. Go on, try your 'at on. No, not like that. Pull if forward a bit. Sailors went out two years ago. That's better. It only needs dusting off a bit, that fur-felt catches every speck, and I'll tell you what, love, I'll lend you me bit of fox to put round your neck. I've never been up 'cemetery yet but what it wasn't blowing fit to freeze your bits and pieces.'

Then his mother's murmur, so low that it was impossible to catch what she was saying. Stanley strained to catch the words without being in the least interested, then stared through the window again.

The sun had gone in and the woman sunbathing folded her deck-chair and carried it inside the house, followed by the cat with its tail erect. A lowering cloud appeared to be so thick that he felt if pressed it would drip apple juice, like the muslin bag his mother sometimes suspended over the big blue bowl in the kitchen when she made apple jelly. His head felt as if someone were adding little sums up in it, pressing with the point of a pencil on every single figure. The thought of life going on, just as the minister had predicted it would, in that house, with the door of Ruby's room closed, her narrow bed stripped of its covers, the wire behind its cretonne curtain bare of her dresses, filled him with a terrible, blank despair. He dipped the pen in the blue-black ink and tried to write a poem about the awfulness of everything. Wrote three lines then tore it up and dropped the pieces into the empty biscuit tin he used as a waste bin.

'You just write me a list of what you want me to get, and I'll go down the market,' he told his mother. 'I won't take the basket, I'll fold a carrier-bag and carry it underneath my arm,' he said, and was touched almost to the point of tears to see how what could have passed for a smile crossed her face.

'Your dad will never be dead as long as you're alive, Stanley,' she said. 'He wouldn't carry a basket neither, not for love nor money he wouldn't. I remember once he brought me a bunch of violets home on a Saturday when

106

he'd been to watch the Rovers, and he stuffed them into his mac pocket rather than carry them through the street.' She licked the point of her pencil and thought for a moment. 'It didn't do them no good neither, but I put them in water with an aspirin and they come up just as good as new.' She sighed. 'It's no good. I can't get my mind on food. It doesn't seem right that we have to eat somehow. I'll give you three shillings and you can get just what you think fit. There'll be cut oranges and bruised tomatoes if you go now . . . oh love, it's all wrong that we should be feeling hungry or bothering about anything when Ruby's . . . when she's not coming through that door no more. I still can't believe it somehow.'

'You'll start feeling better after the funeral on Monday,' Stanley said, then immediately wondered what had made him say such a damn fool thing?

'If anyone else tells me once more that time will heal I'll be like Nellie Crawley and spit in their eye,' his mother had said only the day before. But what else was there to say but platitudes and trite remarks? What *did* one say to the newly bereaved? Stanley folded the carrier-bag into acceptable masculine folds and tucked it beneath his arm.

'You'll be all right till I get back, then?'

Then, as she nodded, he bent his head and kissed her awkwardly on her cheek, knowing that had been quite the wrong thing to do as he saw the rush of tears to her eyes.

'Grief should bring closeness,' he told himself as he walked quickly with head bent forward as usual down the street.

'Everyone can master a grief but he that has it,' he muttered, then as he crossed the street: 'Old Shakespeare had the right words for everything – the old rascal didn't miss a trick.'

'Everyone can master a grief but he that has it,' he said again, causing two women who knew him to turn to each other and say how sad it was that what had happened in the Corporation Park to that poor boy's sister had obviously turned his mind.

'Talking to *himself*,' they told their respective husbands over their Saturday tea of a quarter of tripe – off the seam.

'I'll go down town and pick the brooch up for you if you'd like me to,' Dorothy told her mother. 'Then you won't need to worry about me not getting enough exercise. I'll run all the way down Steep Brow,' she added with the air of one who is dispensing a great favour.

As usual Phyllis tried hard not to sigh at her younger daughter. They were in the front garden and she was down on her knees on a small cushion kept specially for the purpose. She wore her gardening outfit, an old tweed skirt, a long cardigan and a shady hat, although the sun was no more than a watery trickle of light through low-slung clouds. With hands encased in a pair of leather gauntlet gloves she was planting pansy clumps in a neat and well-ordered row, planting them at equal distances from each other, pulling at their foliage until she felt they were roughly the same size, and patting the earth down around them with neat, precise, little pats. Like the contents of the house itself, her garden was the epitome of order and neatness. As one blue vase on one side of the mantelpiece was flanked by its twin on the other, so the shrubs and flowers in Phyllis's garden bloomed in matching identical pairs. If a rose bush came into flower at one side of the velvet lawn, then its counterpart came into matching bloom on the other. In their due seasons the tulips marched down the border like well-drilled soldiers, the daffodils grew in evenly spaced precision to uniform heights, and the privet hedge looked as if it had been manufactured and not grown.

'If she didn't think it was common she'd have got Philips to clip out a couple of ducks at each side of the gate,' Dorothy had told Stanley once when they were playing their favourite game of analysing her parents.

'With identical twin gnomes fishing in matching ponds in the middle of the lawn,' Stanley had said. 'It's a sign of insecurity, you see, Dorothy. Two means more, double means twice the normal.'

'I see,' Dorothy had said, not seeing at all.

Sitting back on her heels Phyllis eyed her with resignation.

'Why you couldn't have gone with Margaret to the tennis club I don't know. Gerald's picking her up there later because he doesn't want her to walk back through the field way alone.' She shook her head as if in sorrow. 'When I was your age I spent every single minute of every single Saturday at the tennis club. I never mooned about doing nothing the way you do.' She got up from her knees and stared with something akin to distaste at the soil on the tips of her gloved fingers. 'Well, I suppose you *could* pick my brooch up for me. Mr Adamson did promise to have it ready today, and I want to wear my grey striped blouse for bridge this evening. It looks nothing without my cameo at the neck.' She looked down at her arm as if expecting to see one of her leather handbags looped neatly into position. 'Never mind the money, just tell Mr Adamson to charge it to us. Goodness knows we've spent enough money there lately with the engagement presents and the silver knife for cutting the cake, not to mention the crucifixes for the bridesmaids.' She knelt down again and trimmed off a leaf which had grown out of proportion to the others. 'It was only the safety chain that needed mending.' Then, trying hard to sound casual, she said: 'Where are you going this evening, dear?'

'I *was* going to the pictures with Stanley,' Dorothy told her, feeling that, under the tragic circumstances, lies in that direction would be in bad taste. 'But he doesn't feel he should go anywhere until after the funeral.' She raised her voice in an attempt at bravado. 'I was going to say that I was going with Mavis and Edna, two girls in my form, but I've promised Father I'll stop telling lies about meeting Stanley.'

Phyllis allowed herself an upwards sideway glance. Her daughter looked very virtuous standing there in her pleated skirt, with the Peter-Pan collar of her white blouse turned down over the collar of her school blazer. Almost as if she were blaming them for her former deceit, Phyllis thought, stabbing furiously into the soil with her index finger.

'Your father's going to the funeral on Monday to represent the *mill*,' Phyllis said, with the emphasis on the word that counted. 'Gerald was going with him but he's stood down to let Mr Sowerbutts go in his place. Margaret says he can't bear to discuss it. He's a sensitive young man, you've only to look at his face to see that he suffers inwardly. Probably because of his sad beginnings.'

'My heart bleeds,' Dorothy said underneath her breath as she walked away down the path, leaving her mother muttering feverishly into a seedling. . . .

She wasn't, Phyllis decided, going to raise the issue at the moment about this dreadful boy from Inkerman Street. Let them get his poor sister decently buried first, then she'd make Matthew listen. Knowing Dorothy as she was sure she did, it was more than likely that the whole sordid business had tinged the friendship with an aura of glamour. Dramatized it into something brave and wonderful. Made Dorothy feel she must stick by him no matter what. She stood up, dragged the cushion a few feet to the right and knelt down again. Now it seemed that he was refusing to go back to school and talking about giving up his place at university. Mrs Wilkinson had heard it from a friend of a friend. And if he left school, what then?

She probed daintily in the cuttings box as if she were selecting a chocolate cream and being careful not to take a hard one by mistake. At eighteen he was too old to take up an apprenticeship that might give him a trade in his fingers, even if there were any openings at the present time. And with nothing but book learning to offer, academic qualifications not backed up by a degree or any training for one of the professions, he would probably end up signing on at the Labour Exchange. Hanging about outside with his hands in his pockets, just one more statistic in what the papers

110

called the economic graveyard of lost hopes. She knelt back on her heels, proud of herself for remembering the phrase. Matthew would in all probability offer him a job at the mill, knowing Matthew. But it would have to be a job created especially, with a hundred men standing by for every job available.

The town was full of boys who had never worked, the occasional packet of cigarettes and a daily meeting at the billiard halls being the only pleasure in their drab lives. Oh, she read the papers all right, and listened to Matthew when he was up on his soap-box. The very street in which that boy lived – she could not bring herself even to *think* his name – existed merely because it had been built originally as cottages, well, terraced houses for the mill workers. She stood up and rubbed at an aching knee.

And if this grisly thing hadn't happened, he would have gone off to university at the end of the summer, and out of sight would surely have meant out of mind. She walked stiff-legged into the house, seeing, in her mind's eye, a clear picture of herself having to tell Mrs Wilkinson that Mrs Armstrong was coming to tea. She saw Dorothy helping that boy to carry a basket of washing through the streets; saw her bridge friends sniggering behind their cards. Saw it all, and was depressed beyond measure.

Dorothy was thinking about Stanley so thoroughly that she didn't see her cousin until they were almost nose to nose.

'I've been playing tennis in the park,' Beryl told her unnecessarily, swinging her racket with three tennis balls in a green net wound round the handle. 'Talk about being lovesick. You're as bad as Gerald, you are.' She lowered her voice, although the tree-lined road was completely deserted. 'I swore I wouldn't tell a living soul, but he's lost one of the cuff-links Margaret bought him. I was on the landing after lunch, and I saw him searching his room. He was opening drawers and then banging them shut. He was even looking underneath the carpet and feeling with his hand to see if they'd rolled there somehow. I asked him what he was looking for, and he jumped a mile. Then he told me how terrible he felt about losing them with Margaret buying them for him and everything. He said it made him quite sick just thinking about it as they were more precious to him than the King's crown.' She sighed. 'Isn't that romantic? You won't tell a living soul about it, will you? I've only told you because I think it's so beautiful.'

'As if I would,' Dorothy said, backing away. If she didn't hurry up the shops would be closed.

But Beryl hadn't finished. 'As a matter of fact I saw him in the park just now, walking along a path with his nose nearly touching the ground. But I didn't let on. He thinks I spy on him, for some reason.' Her plain face shone with perspiration beneath the wide brim of her school panama. 'It's real spooky in the park. There's a piece of tarpaulin over the place where you know what. Me and Connie – she's the girl I've been playing tennis with, and she beat me again, you might know – we went to look. Isn't it awful about that girl who got killed having a baby? Mother says . . .'

'I can't stop,' Dorothy said quickly. 'I've got to catch the shops before they shut. See you in church tomorrow morning?'

'Suppose so,' Beryl said. 'And you won't split about what I've just told you? I think you're beastly rotten about Gerald, if you want to know. He says he trusts me and that when they're married I can go and stay the night with them sometimes.' She walked away, the tennis racket banging disconsolately against her fat legs sprouting from white ankle socks, leaving Dorothy feeling, as usual, vaguely ashamed, and with the feeling that she could have been kinder. Cousin Beryl will be making people feel guilty all her life, she reasoned, with a sudden flash of perception.

She blushed and turned her head away as three boys standing on a street corner whistled after her. She could

112

almost bring herself to feel sorry for Gerald Tomlin having
to live under Beryl's constant vigilance.

She was half way down Steep Brow when she suddenly
remembered that Gerald had *found* the cuff-links; that he
had been wearing them the night before. At least they had
looked like the same. But had they? She remembered standing at the door and waving them off to the dance, Margaret
in her garden-swing dress, and Gerald in what her father
always called his penguin trappings. She had thought then
that the cuff-links appeared to be smaller than the original
ones. She stepped off a kerb and stumbled, causing a man at
the tram-stop to say 'whoops-a-daisy'. And if he had found
them why was he still searching? And why was he searching
in the *park*?

Her mind raced ahead so that she walked along, seeing
nothing of the busy Saturday afternoon crowds, hearing
nothing as the trams rumbled by. *If* Gerald had lost the
cuff-links he could have replaced them. He could have gone
back to the jeweller's shop and bought a similar pair. He
could have done it to spare Margaret the knowledge that he
had lost her present to him. He could have. Of course he
could have. She bumped into a pram and was loudly told to
look where she was going by the baby's mother.

But if he'd done that, why was he still searching his
room? Lifting the carpet, according to Beryl. And why was
he in the park walking along with his head bent? Gerald
Tomlin didn't go for walks in the park. Gerald Tomlin
didn't walk anywhere, the red sports car being almost an
extension of himself. Someone called out a 'hallo', but she
glanced through them, showing no recognition. Yes, the
searching beneath the carpet in Gerald's room could mean
that he couldn't bear to think he had misplaced the original
pair on account of their sentimental value. Mother was
always saying what a lovely romantic streak Gerald had in
him. 'Not like a northern man with his mind filled with

113

nothing else but beer and football,' she'd said more than once.

And Margaret herself had said how upset he was at losing the cuff-links. So upset that he wanted it kept a secret. But Gerald had what Mrs Wilkinson's magazines called 'charm'. He would, or at least he *could* have said that he'd lost them and elicited sympathy, not irritation. Gerald Tomlin always managed to come out the hero, usually the suave Ronald Colman type hero, in every story he told against himself. And charming people did tell stories against themselves just to make themselves appear all the more charming. That was another truth about people she had found out for herself, and one she must tell to Stanley when next they met.

'Tolstoy is the only writer who can hold up a mirror to a man's soul,' Stanley had said, and gone on to say that was the kind of writer he would be one day when he was qualified to earn money, to take time off to write.

Dorothy turned into King Edward Street without the faintest recollection of having got there, was surprised to find herself standing outside Mr Adamson's jeweller's shop, and stood for a moment staring at the rows of diamond rings in the side window, each one mounted on a velvet pad with the price neatly tabulated underneath. One ring costing a hundred and fifty pounds had diamonds as big as peas, and even in her state of mental agitation she found that she was pursing up her lips in a gesture of disbelief.

The door-bell pinged as she went inside, and Mr Adamson's Saturday lady, a plump treble-chinned girl of about thirty with a black dress stretched tightly over her pouter-pigeon bosom, came forward.

'Can I help you?'

Dorothy bit her lip and glanced over to the side counter where Mr Adamson was setting out rings on a mat of black velvet, showing them off to an obviously embarrassed young man and an obviously triumphant girl who was insisting on trying on each ring and holding up her hand to the light to check them for sparkle. The jeweller, one of Matthew Bolton's Rotary friends, was leaning forward, explaining about built-up shoulders and claw settings, smiling like a benevolent Father Christmas on the young couple, and telling them to take their time.

'Take your time about it,' he was saying at that very moment. 'It's only once.' Then he laughed and stroked his mutton-chop whiskers. 'Or at least we hope it's only once.'

The couple giggled and leaned on each other, and Dorothy spoke, softly to the assistant.

'I'll wait for Mr Adamson, if you don't mind. It's personal.'

'As you wish, miss.'

The Saturday lady sniffed with a sideways twitch of nostrils and walked with a rather offended tripping step into a room at the back, where through a small window Dorothy saw her light a cigarette and blow a thin stream of smoke up to the ceiling as if to disconnect herself from the whole matter.

Yes, if Gerald Tomlin *had* replaced the lost cuff-links for a new pair, it would have still been quite feasible that he would go on searching for the originals. And the normal place, the most *likely* place, would be his bedroom. Nothing was more annoying than losing something and having no idea where one has lost it. Father was always losing a cuff-link or a collar stud.

'A place for everything,' Mother would say, 'and everything in its place, and no, Matthew, Mrs Wilkinson has not moved them. She dusts round everything, even the lace covers on your tall-boy, as well I know.'

Dorothy stood on one leg and sighed deeply. But if her father couldn't find what he was looking for in his room, would he be likely to go searching for it in the *park*? Walking along the paths with his head bent, searching, pretending he was just out for an afternoon stroll, but in reality searching? Along the side paths, the long, winding paths leading to the duck pond, the place where. . . .

Yes, it had been Beryl's mention of seeing Gerald in the park that had made the warning bells ring.

Dorothy sat down with a sudden thump on the horse-hair-covered chair placed there for customers with weak legs or hearts. Her own legs felt as if they had started to melt, and her heart was beating with loud and heavy thuds somewhere it had no right to be.

She was getting carried away, as her mother would say. She was as usual allowing her imagination to run off with itself. Even her last school report under General Comments had said that she should try to hold her imagination on a tighter rein.

She took a handkerchief with a bunch of flowers embroidered on one corner out of her blazer pocket and blew her nose on an uncomfortable French knot, and when Mr Adamson spoke to her she jumped as if someone had shot a poisoned arrow into her back.

'By the left, Dorothy, but you were far away,' she heard Mr Adamson say. 'That's three times I've spoken to you, chuck, and you haven't heard a word.' His large face beamed concern. 'Would you like a drink of water, love? You've gone right pale and no mistake.'

Dorothy tried a shaky smile.

'Just thinking, Mr Adamson, that's all. Honestly, I'm fine.'

The jeweller wasn't convinced. 'Hope you're not sickening for this flu, chuck. There's a lot of it about. Your auntie was in only a few days back and we had to sit your cousin out at the back on a chair. Green as grass she were. It's a treacherous month May is; one minute you think it's springlike, and then the next it's as parky as the middle of winter.'

'My cousin Beryl is always sitting outside shops on chairs,' Dorothy said, and he laughed a surprisingly thin laugh for so big a man.

'Come in for your mother's brooch, have you then,

116

chuck? It's all ready wrapped up for her, and you can tell her it's on the house. It were nobbut the pin at the back needed replacing.' He reached underneath the counter and produced a small parcel. 'Soon be the wedding, won't it? My wife's nearly driving me mad talking about what she's going to wear. Who's going to look at *you*, I keep saying, but it makes no difference. She's out now with a piece of stuff in her handbag trying to find a pair of shoes what matches.'

Dorothy picked up the parcel and put it in her blazer pocket. Her fingers tightened round it as she tried to make her voice sound casual.

'Nobody at our house talks about anything else but the wedding.' She hesitated, then plunged on. 'You've met our Margaret's fiancé, haven't you, Mr Adamson? He's a very nice person, isn't he?'

'Out of the top drawer right enough, chuck.'

Dorothy glanced around her in desperation. The door-bell tinkled and as a woman with a loaded shopping basket came into the shop the Saturday assistant came out from the back with her little tripping step.

'The cuff-links,' Dorothy said feverishly. 'The ones Margaret bought him for their engagement present. . . ?' Her voice tailed away as she realized her chance was almost gone. Already the woman customer was glancing over in their direction, making it quite clear that she, too, wished to be served by Mr Adamson, and the assistant's nostrils were dilating in disgust.

Then, as Dorothy was to tell Stanley afterwards, fate intervened.

The jeweller leaned forward confidentially.

'So you're in on the secret, are you then, chuck?'

Dorothy nodded, holding her breath.

'Lovely thought to come in here and buy a replacement for the ones he'd misplaced. Long before he'd had a proper chance to look for them, really. "She mustn't know," he kept saying, and I was only too happy to find him a pair almost the same but a bit bigger.' He winked. 'Good business for me and a perfect solution for him, though I have said of course that should the others turn up I'll take them back. Knowing your father so well and everything.'

The assistant came over, and with her black-clad bosom a mere few inches away from the jeweller's gaze, whispered to him.

'You'll have to excuse me, Dorothy love,' he said, then placed a podgy finger over his mouth. 'Mum's the word now. All right?'

'All right,' Dorothy said, and walked from the shop, her smile as false as the string of pearls Mr Adamson kept draped over the silver-framed photograph of himself in his mayoral robes of three years before.

It was as if something she had always known but never admitted had suddenly taken shape in her mind. As if the reason for her instinctive and unexplained aversion to Gerald Tomlin had suddenly been justified. As if Grandpa Bolton had suddenly materialized, telling her that first impressions were usually the right ones. She could still recall the feeling of distaste when she had first met Gerald's shiny blue gaze.

She walked slowly away from the shop, past the Home and Colonial Store with its smell of freshly ground coffee, at that very moment being poured into little dark brown bags by the counter assistants in their clerical grey cotton coats. Past Blake's café with its tray of cream fancies displayed downstairs, and its winding staircase leading to the upper floor, where the well-to-do matrons of the town met on market days for a pot of tea and a well-buttered sultana scone.

On across the road to the market place, with the stall-holders already packing their unsold wares; past the open entrance to the fish market, with its overpowering smell assailing her senses.

Walking slowly, seeing nothing, thoughts too complex for understanding zooming round and round in her mind

118

like a moth caught in a basin-type light fitting. Actually muttering aloud, halting and giving a small cry of alarm as she felt a sudden light touch on her arm.

And seeing Stanley standing before her, tall and pale, with a carrier-bag held shamefacedly in his hand, a head of celery and sticks of rhubarb protruding from it.

Eleven

There was something essentially sensual, primitive and wanton about all the mounds of fruit and vegetables so lavishly displayed on the market stalls, Stanley had always thought. Especially as he had calculated that only roughly a quarter of the town's population could actually afford to spend with any kind of freedom. There was a family up at the top of his street with a father who had been out of work for eight years. His mother had told him once that they ate meat (a shilling's worth of stewing beef) only once a week, and drank out of condensed milk tins.

'Tea, tinned milk, margarine, bread and potatoes,' his mother had said was all they ate. 'Six children and another on the way, and bugs crawling over the bedroom walls. She's stopped even *trying* to keep the place clean.'

Food as luscious as locusts, he thought bitterly as he waited in a small queue at the salad stall, watching the quarters of shiny dark green watercress and tender spiked lettuce leaves being lowered on to the wide scales. Pale firm tomatoes, blood-red radishes, green-tufted spring onions, and beetroots steaming from a recent boiling. And right behind him the fruit and vegetable stalls. Oranges piled in tempting pyramids, red Delicious apples, with the ones at the front polished to a shining brightness. Potpourris of root vegetables ready bunched together for the stock-pot, and tiny new potatoes needing only a rub of the thumb to rid them of their thin skins.

Food for the gods; food to enjoy, to sink your teeth into a

juicy pear, to taste the soft white flesh . . . He remembered the way Ruby would bite into an apple when his mother came back from the market on Wednesdays and Saturdays. Wiping it first, then biting with her sharp little teeth, eating it right to the core, pips and all. To his dismay he felt the sting of tears behind his eyes.

Then to control himself he fingered the money in his pocket, doing little sums in his mind, as carefully as any conscientious housewife.

Past the fruit stalls, at the very edge of the market, with their little tables set out on the pavement, he could see the shrimp women from Southport in their flowered pinafores and their poke-bonnets, with the tiny pots of buttered shrimps set in rows. He nodded to himself . . . He must somehow work out his budget so that there was enough money left to buy a pot for his mother. Funny the way he kept on thinking about his father since it happened. With force of habit he tuned into his subconscious. Maybe it was because he was trying, in his own way, to stand in for his father in an attempt to help his mother? Trying to think what the quiet man would have said, would have done.

Every Saturday dinner-time, on his way home from work, his father had stopped at the shrimp women's tables and bought his wife a pot of the pink tiny shrimps crowded together beneath their solidified lid of butter. And on a good week he would add a carton of rum butter, gritty with sugar, warm tasting, a reminder of her Cumberland up-bringing.

Oat-cakes drying on the rack, shrimps in a pot, and rum butter spread thickly on the toast. Saturday evening round the inevitable coal fire, with Ruby sitting on the rug between her father's knees as he rubbed her newly washed hair dry. Dark, springy, curly hair, that he would never recall without seeing that leaf caught up in it as she lay on a slab at the mortuary with a sheet over her naked body. He swallowed hard on the lump in his throat, a lump as big as a hard-boiled egg.

'A quarter of loose lettuce leaves and one medium-sized beetroot,' he told the white-coated woman behind the stall, then counted his change carefully before passing on to the fruit and vegetable stalls, where, after concentrated comparisons, he bought a cauliflower, and noted with satisfaction that the rhubarb was reduced in price in deference to the lateness of the afternoon.

And there was enough, just enough money left for a pot of shrimps. He fingered the coin in his pocket, exchanging it already in his mind for the tiny white pot, noting with relief that the shrimp women were still sitting at their tables, poke-bonnets nodding as they counted out their day's takings.

Then turning swiftly in the right direction he came face to face with Dorothy.

'Well, hallo,' they said together, then said it again, blushing to the roots of their respective hair-lines, staring at each other in delighted amazement, as if their meeting was unexpected enough to qualify as a miracle.

'I've been shopping for me mum, for me mother,' Stanley said, explaining away the shame-making carrier-bag.

'Me too,' Dorothy told him, patting her pocket, then she put out a hand and gripped his arm tightly. 'Stanley, seeing you like this was meant to be. Honestly.' She glanced quickly from him to the milling crowds of late shoppers thronging the narrow alley-way between the stalls. 'I've got to talk to you. It's about your – it's about your Ruby. I've found something out, but we can't talk about it here.' She lowered her voice dramatically. 'It's awfully serious. Honestly.'

Stanley fingered the single coin in his jacket pocket, and without a moment's hesitation suggested that they went into the nearby Market Place and had a cup of tea at the railed-off cafeteria set amidst the stalls. Well, his mum would never know that she had nearly had a pot of shrimps for her tea, would she? And the rhubarb had been a decided bargain. What he'd lost on the roundabout he had gained on the swings, so to speak. It was all relative, he told himself as they walked side by side into the covered Market Place, past the stalls laden with Miss Muffet prints, sixpence a yard, the bales of unbleached calico, the edge-whipped flannelette sheets, the pink and blue directoire knickers, the winceyette nightgowns, the combinations displayed with embarrassing showmanship.

And the small cafeteria was deserted, the two girls behind the counter busily wiping down the wide surface with damp cloths.

'You sit here,' Stanley said, hiding the carrier-bag beneath a table, and going over to the counter.

'We're just shutting,' a girl with dolly-rouged cheeks told him, and he blushed and laid the coin on the damp counter.

'Two teas, please,' he said firmly.

'I said we're just shutting,' the girl told him again.

He looked her straight in the eye. 'It's not half-past five yet, and we won't be long. You don't have to brew a fresh pot. All right?'

Sighing, she picked up the huge brown tea-pot and slopped tea into two thick white cups.

'Does your mam know you're out then?' she said, and her friend said, 'Shut your gob, Mavis. Never let it be said that we stood in the way of love's young dream, eh?'

Blushing so that his ears glowed pink, Stanley looked round to see whether Dorothy had heard, but she was sitting hunched over the table with a look of such misery etched on her face, that when he sat down opposite to her, he stretched out a hand and gently stroked her cheek. The girl with rouged circles on her round cheeks grinned and drew a heart in the air with an arrow through it for her friend.

'Juliet and her bloody Romeo,' she said, and they giggled together as if it were the joke of the year.

'What is it then that's so important?' Stanley said, pushing a big glass bowl of sugar in Dorothy's direction.

She shook her head. 'I don't take it. Oh, Stanley, it's so awful I don't know how to begin.'

He ladled three spoonfuls into his own cup. 'Well, try, then. Come on.'

She lowered her voice to a soft whisper. 'I've found out that Gerald Tomlin, you know, the chap our Margaret's going to marry next month – oh God, I've found out that he could have been somehow involved with your sister. With your Ruby.'

Stanley stopped stirring the sugar round in the thick dark tea and let the spoon clatter back into the saucer. 'Say that again.'

'He . . . well, he lost a pair of cuff-links, and made a great to-do of swearing our Margaret to secrecy, and then he said he'd found them, but I've just been in Adamson's jeweller's, and I tricked Mr Adamson into telling me that Gerald hadn't found them at all; that he went into the shop and bought another pair almost the same. As much like the first pair to fool Margaret anyway.'

Stanley blinked, picked up his cup, drank from it, discovered it was only lukewarm and put it down again. Always quick to see the point of any statement immediately, he would have smiled had it not been for the look of intense misery on Dorothy's face. He answered her with caution.

'But how does that tie in with our Ruby? What I mean to say is, how does the fact that he lost a pair of cuff-links, and if he lost them from his shirt he would only lose *one*, surely? And wouldn't it be a quite natural thing to do to try to replace them rather than upset your Margaret? I suppose she bought them for him in the first place, then?'

Dorothy nodded. 'They were her engagement present to him.'

'Then where's the mystery?'

She bit her lip and spoke so quietly that he had to lean towards her, almost to lip-read to decipher what she said next.

'But he's *still* looking for them. Desperately searching for them – or one of them – as if he wasn't sure where he'd lost them, or it, and as if it was vitally important that he found out. He was lifting the carpet in his bedroom. My cousin Beryl spies on him because she has a crush on him, and she saw him, and as far as I can make out he got flustered and told her not to tell anyone. But she couldn't resist telling me not half an hour ago because Beryl doesn't get secrets told to her you see.'

Stanley tried to see. 'Well, I can understand him lifting the carpet. Maybe he's the kind of person who can't bear to lose things. I'm a bit like that myself. If they'd rolled off the bed or off his tall-boy, then under the carpet is a perfectly normal place to look. I honestly don't follow . . .'

Dorothy's blue eyes narrowed to slits. 'Ah, but listen to this. Beryl also saw him later this afternoon. After she'd finished a game of tennis. Stanley . . . he was in the park, walking along with his head bent, obviously still searching. He's just not the kind of bloke who goes for walks in the park. For walks anywhere. He takes that car of his even if he's only going a hundred yards down the road.' She ran a finger round the rim of her cup. 'And that's not all. I think I've known all along that he was seeing, well . . . taking some of the girl weavers out from father's mill. Before he got engaged to our Margaret, I'll give him that. And he tells lies. He's a pathological liar if you want my opinion. He told me he only knew your Ruby to nod to, but I remembered in bed last night that once when I went down to the mill – oh, months ago, I saw him talking to her. It was probably about work. I never thought any more about it, till last night, and even then it didn't seem to matter. But now . . .' she lifted her eyes.

'Go on.'

'Well, he talked to me one day when he ran me home in his car, and he was trying to tell me something.' She frowned in concentration. 'He was trying to win me over to his side, to tell me that whatever he'd done before, none of it was of any importance now that he'd fallen in love with Margaret, and was going to marry her. Real sob stuff. No, don't say anything. I'm talking it out in my mind. It's more a *feeling* I have about him, a something I've sensed ever since he came. He's a *cad*, that's the right word. Or at least he was. Now . . . well, I don't know . . . And since the murder he's changed. He's badly frightened, I know he is. He didn't want to go to the Police Ball, and he's got out of going to the funeral on Monday. Mother would say I'm letting my imagination run away with me as usual, but it's a creepy sort of premonition I have when he's around, and when Beryl said she'd seen him in the park this afternoon, well it all clicked into place.'

She fell silent, and Stanley stared at her, feeling the same way he had when an over-enthusiastic team-mate in the school football team had kicked the ball straight at him and winded him. He didn't know what to say, and yet his mind, the part of his brain that was being trained academically to deduce, to pick out the salient points in a discussion and discard the rest, was working overtime. For a long moment they sat there, opposite to each other, with the thick white cups on the smeared table in front of them, knees touching, looking into each other's faces, marooned there in the busy Market Hall as if they had been marooned on a secluded and secret island.

'So we'll have to go to the police,' she said at last.

'No!' Stanley's voice was husky as if he was recovering from a cold. 'No, Dorothy.' He reached for her hands and then stared down at them joined together with his own. 'It's too soon. There's not enough. It's not even what they would call circumstantial evidence.' He held on and she tried to break away. 'Listen! You can't do that to your family. Think what it would mean. He may have met Ruby, he may well have been seeing her, but apart from the bit about Beryl seeing him in the park . . .'

'Walking along with his head bent.'

He nodded. 'But I always walk with *my* head bent. My mother's always telling me off about it. Apart from that, there isn't a thing really to pin on him, not a thing.'

She managed to pull away from him this time, her cheeks flushing with anger.

'But it all fits. Can't you see? It's like a jigsaw puzzle in my head, with every piece fitting into place.' She actually beat at her forehead with a clenched fist. 'You told me yourself that Ruby had been unnaturally secretive, and of course she would be. A girl like Ruby would be, well . . . like putty in his hands. He's what they call a charmer, Stanley, you don't know him like I do. You don't know him at all.' Her voice rose. 'He's devious, that's what he is. Devious and slimy and shiny and a *liar*. But I'll say this for him, I really do believe that when he got engaged to Margaret he stopped seeing other girls. I really believe he intended to be faithful to her, and it might have been like that, but when Ruby found she was having a baby, found out for sure, she had to see him to tell him, and she persuaded him to see her just once, and when she told him he panicked and . . . and killed her!'

Stanley shook his head from side to side. Like a stupid tortoise, she thought wildly. Sitting there with that stupid carrier-bag at his feet, with that stupid stick of rhubarb sticking out of it, and his head shaking from side to side. As if he hadn't taken in a word she was saying. As if it wasn't his sister lying dead in the Chapel of Rest waiting to be buried in the windy cemetery in two days' time.

'I'm going,' she said, getting up and walking quickly away from him, leaving him sitting there as if he'd been struck dumb, with the two girls behind the counter watching her go with fascinated interest.

And there they were, as Mrs Wilkinson was to tell her husband that tea-time, Mrs Bolton's younger daughter, Dorothy, and that Stanley Armstrong out of Inkerman Street. Chasing one another out of the Market Place, him calling her name out loud, and her crying if she hadn't been mistaken. Just like a couple of kids out of Foundry Street, who wouldn't be expected to behave any better.

'You could have knocked me down with a feather,' she

was to say. 'I saw them with my own two eyes as I was taking the short cut down the back steps to the tram stop. "Dorothy! Don't go. Wait for me!" he was shouting at the very top of his voice, and her running and crying. Her mother would have had a pink fit if she could have seen her daughter showing herself up in public. And you'd have thought he would have had more respect for the dead, carrying on like that with his sister not even decently buried.'

'Nowt but a lovers' tiff,' Ned said, more interested in what was for his tea.

And Stanley would have overtaken Dorothy's flying figure easily, but at the entrance to the Market Place he had to pull himself up sharp to prevent knocking over a small boy with an ice-cream cornet in his hand.

'Where's the fire?' a tall man said, scooping the child up out of his way. 'It'll be over afore tha gets there if tha's not quick about it.'

Calling an apology over his shoulder, Stanley ran on, catching up with Dorothy at the foot of the wide flight of stone steps leading into the Town Hall building.

With his free hand he grabbed at her wrist, but she jerked away from him and hurried on, walking quickly, talking to him out of the corner of her mouth.

'You want to know what I feel like, Stanley Armstrong?' she said as if he had asked her. 'I feel as if you've just thrown a bucket of cold water over me, if you want to know.'

He saw a stick of rhubarb about to fall to the ground and shoved it back into the carrier-bag, and seeing him do it was illogically, to Dorothy, the last straw.

'You care more about that stick of rhubarb than what I've just told you. You don't believe a single word of it, do you?' When he didn't answer, she said loudly. 'I don't swear, but bloody hell. Hell's bloody bells.'

He put out his hand towards her again, but she knocked it away with a fierce little swipe.

'Dorothy listen!'

'You listen to me and I'll listen to you. It's your own sister we're talking about, remember?'

She was walking so quickly she was almost tripping over her feet, refusing to look at him, almost beside herself with exasperation. He had never seen her other than passively what Mrs Crawley would have called 'lady-like', and her excitement was catching. They were approaching the bottom of Steep Brow now, and suddenly, heedless of the stares of passers-by, he caught her arm in a grip so firm she was forced to stop. He swung her round to face him, and the expression in his dark eyes was so intense, so pleading, that her angry words died away.

'I've got to go back now, Dorothy. I can't walk home with you shouting at me like this, even if I wanted to. I promised I wouldn't be out long, and me mother's in such a state I have to watch out for her all the time. But after tea tonight, Mrs Crawley's coming in to sit with her, and I'll come round. I'll come up to your house about half-past seven. I'll stand at the corner of your road, and I'll wait for you, and we'll find somewhere to go and talk about it. All right?'

His voice was quiet and controlled, but his manner was as aggressive as if he were shouting at the top of his voice. 'And in the meantime you keep it to yourself.' He went on in that deceptively calm voice; 'My God, Dorothy, how do you think I feel? If there's even a scrap of truth in what you say, I won't be able to keep my hands off him. But it's dangerous talk. It's worse than dangerous.' He shook her arm none too gently. 'If we can prove that he was seeing our Ruby, then I'll be off to the police station so quick you won't see me for dust. That satisfy you?'

Dorothy sighed deeply. She felt tired and beaten, bewildered and lost. She drew in a great intake of breath. 'All right then, but you don't need to wait at the corner of the road. Leave it till eight o'clock, and I'll be alone in the house. I'm tired of standing on corners, Stanley, and I never want to sit on a bench with you in the park again.' She shuddered. 'I might tell them you're coming round and I might not. It all depends.' She turned to walk away from him, and before he set off in the opposite direction, he stood and watched her go.

But she didn't turn round, just walked away, her hands deep in the pockets of her blazer, her feet trailing as if she was in no hurry to go home, in no hurry to go anywhere at all.

Twelve

'I've been down to the selling-out shop and fetched four bottles of stout,' Mrs Crawley said, almost before her head came round the door. 'So get the poker in quick, Mrs Armstrong, and we'll waste no time in giving it a bit of bite.'

Ada did as she was told. She thrust the long poker with its brass handle into the glowing fire, positioning it between the bars of the grate, and watched as Nellie Crawley took off her headscarf and coat, draping them over the back of a chair. She moves about this house as if she's lived here all her life, she thought, not unkindly. It was queer how things turned out. She didn't even have to get up from her chair to get two pots from the scullery. Nellie Crawley knew where they were.

'Don't move, love,' she was saying. 'I'll see to it. By heck but it's cold out. Him as said "Ne'er cast a clout till May is out" knew what he were saying. I didn't cast me vest all last summer, and I doubt if I'll be doing it this. Best place to be is round the fire on a night like this. I've got goose-pimples on me goose-pimples if tha wants to know.'

Ada smiled briefly. If anyone had told her that in such a short time she would have come to know, and aye, – why not say it? – come to *love* the loud-mouthed blowsy woman from across the street, she would have said they were daft. Coarse Nellie Crawley might be, as 'common as muck' folks in the street said, but she didn't know what she'd have done without her these past few days.

'Here we are then, love, one for thee and t'other for me.'

Nellie set two pint mugs down on the hearth, and smiled. 'That'll put some lead in tha' pencil, cock.'

Ada nodded. She knew that all things being different, Nellie Crawley would be spending her Saturday evening goodness knows where. Setting off down the street in her black costume, and her pill-box hat with the eye-veil pulled down over her thickly powdered face. Setting off to meet a man? A lover? Or merely to sit in the corner of some public house with a couple of blowsy friends, drinking the hours away till closing-time, leaving her little husband nodding over the fire, listening to the wireless. So they said. It had long been a matter of conjecture in the street as to where Nellie went or what she did on her nights out. But it was none of their business. And none of hers, Ada reminded herself, feeling a twinge of shame as she remembered her own theories as to the kind of woman Nellie Crawley was. 'No better than she should be, and as brazen as brass with it,' she had said herself, on more than one occasion.

Nellie leaned forward, took the poker out of the fire, spat on it and returned it. 'Your Stanley upstairs?'

Ada shook her head. 'He's gone out, Mrs Crawley. I might as well tell you, I'm a bit bothered.' She twisted a corner of her apron round in her fingers. 'He's gone up the park end to see his girl. Matthew Bolton's daughter, our Ruby's boss at the mill.' She gave the poker an extra riddle, turning it round and round in the red embers. 'What her mother thinks about it, I don't rightly know.'

Nellie's voice rose on a squeak of indignation. 'Your Stanley's as good as any of them toffee-nosed sods any old day.'

'I know. Don't get me wrong. I just don't want him to get hurt more than he has been, that's all. It doesn't do. Not that I think owt will come of it; it never works when the money's on the wrong side, and if our Stanley sticks to what he says about not going to the university . . .' She sighed. 'I've persuaded him to bide his time in that direction; there's neither of us thinking straight just now. He were upset about something at tea-time, something more than our Ruby I mean. He'd met that lass down on the market and I think they'd had words. She's bonny enough, but I bet she can be a bit of a tartar. But our Stanley's a sensible lad.'

'And as good as them any old day, Mrs Armstrong. I don't know the lass, not moving in such exalted circles like, but she could do a lot worse for herself than your Stanley, whether he's been to Oxford University or not. If he does leave school he'll not be on the dole for long won't your Stanley, you mark my words.'

'She's only seventeen.'

'Aye, reet enough, but at her age I'd been working for four years and courting strong. More bloody fool me.'

'She's still at school, Mrs Crawley.'

Nellie took the poker out of the fire, nodded with approval at its red and glowing tip, and thrust it into one of the mugs of stout, beaming all over her thin face with satisfaction as the dark brown liquid frothed and hissed over the rim.

'Get that down tha gob, Mrs Armstrong. That'll warm the cockles reet enough, and stop fretting about your Stanley. He'll likely know half a dozen more girls afore he decides to settle down.' She passed over the flowing mug and put the poker back in the fire. 'Don't seem right to me keeping a lass at school when she's a grown woman.' She put her feet on the fender and pulled up her skirt. 'Nowt like warming your bits and pieces in front of a good fire. Aye, I've seen them High School girls, titties bursting out of their gym-slips, making eyes at the boys from the Grammar School. I'll tell you straight, Mrs Armstrong, I don't hold with too much of this education for girls. For boys it's all right, I suppose, if they're clever like your Stanley, but what happens to them girls wagging their behinds in their gym-slips? I'll tell thee. They gets married straight from school, knowing nowt. What good is Shakespeare and that algebra stuff when the babies come along? Tha doesn't need to pass an exam to know how to change a mucky nappy. Come on,

133

get tha feet up aside mine on the fender, and later I'll nip down to the chip shop and fetch us a three and a fourpenny. And no arguing about the money, either. I got me divi last week, and it's burning a hole in me pocket. What's money for if tha can't spend it, I'd like to know.'

Ada's eyes swam with the ever ready tears, and she groped in her apron pocket for a handkerchief. 'I'll never be able to pay you back for what you've done for me these past few days, Mrs Crawley.' She blew her nose hard. 'I had a letter from my brother up in Maryport this morning, and he finds now he won't be able to get down for the funeral Monday morning. It would mean him coming tomorrow, see, and he's frightened to take the time off his work. He says they're looking for excuses to lay men off at the mine, and he has four children still at school.' She sighed deeply. 'We were very close when we were young, but well . . . tha knows how it is. There never seemed the money for the train fare, and over the years we stopped going, and when me husband was alive we didn't seem to need no one else. And since then it's been work and more work. We were such a happy family, the four of us, not always quarrelling and bickering like some folks. And now there's only Stanley and me left. I can' credit it somehow.'

Nellie thrust the poker into the second mug of stout. 'Aye, this fear of coming out o' work makes cowards of us all. I've seen men lie and cheat and do their own kith and kin down to keep a job. My old man's as soft as they come, but he'd make a bargain with owd Nick himself to stay in work. It's getting to the stage when them that has a job feels ashamed. You know summat? I don't get me groceries all at once from the Co-op now. I gets them a few at a time so I don't have to walk up the street with a laden basket.' She tilted her head back and drank deeply, then wiped her mouth with the back of her hand. 'I'll bet they're short of nowt where your Stanley is tonight. I'll bet that Matthew Bolton has never had to want for a bob or two.'

'All the same, I'd have liked our Jim to be at the funeral

Monday,' Ada said, starting to cry again. 'Our Stanley's only a boy; it's too much for him, he's been so wrapped up in his books he hasn't left enough time over for just living, and now it seems all that learning is going to waste.' She choked on a sob.

Nellie patted her knee. 'Have a proper cry if tha feels like it, love. Don't mind me, far better that tha gets it out of tha system now than bottles it up. Worst thing anyone can do is to bottle it all up. I knew a woman once who never cried once when her old man passed over while watching a football match, and six months later to the day she were riddled from head to foot with the arthritis. Couldn't move nowt but her eyeballs. And I'm not going to tell thee that time heals, because it bloody doesn't. All time does is stop it bleeding a bit, that's all.'

'I wish our Stanley had worn his suit to go up there,' Ada said five minutes later. 'But he's gone out in his pullover and a sports jacket that doesn't fit him no more. I'd like him to have looked his best. But they won't listen.'

Then, remembering how Ruby hadn't listened either, she started to cry again, softly, as if there was a well inside her that would never dry up.

'I like your jacket,' Dorothy said insincerely when she opened the front door to Stanley's ring. 'I've never seen it before, have I? Here, give it to me, and I'll hang it up.'

She took it from him, noticing the frayed edges to the cuffs, feeling the rough texture of the cheap material, and, turning round to face him, thought how pale and ill at ease he looked in the green sweater with its V neck showing off a quite hideous red spotted tie. She much preferred him in his school blazer and striped tie, she decided, despising herself even as she thought it.

And as she stared at him, in the few seconds it took for her to see how different, how out of place, he looked against her home background, it came to her that she didn't love him.

Not really *love* him. She liked him, and she wasn't a snob like her mother, heaven forbid, but in that flash of a moment, Dorothy's infatuation, her seventeen-year-old's infatuation for the gangling boy standing beside her, died. And if Phyllis had been able to read her daughter's mind, she would have been silently applauding.

Dorothy was appalled, horrified and bewildered, and to cover her confusion she took him by the hand, and led him down the oak-panelled hall and into the sitting-room.

How was it possible? she was asking herself silently; how was it possible to love someone one minute and then look at him and know that you had been wrong? Was this what her father had meant when he had advised her to take her time? She squeezed Stanley's hand in contrition, pleading with him in her mind for forgiveness.

Stanley stared round him, trying hard not to stare and failing completely. His eyes took in the size of the room, more than twice the size of the living-room at home, the height of the ceiling, the depth of the cushions on the three-piece suite. He blinked at the brightness of the cream-tiled fireplace with its raised hearth and its twinkling brasses. His toe traced the pattern of the thick carpet, and he boggled at the bookshelves let into wide niches at each side of the fireplace. Leather-bound books, in sets, arranged in rows of equal sizes, their bindings matching, looking as if the only time they were taken down was for dusting. He pulled at the knot of the hideous tie as if it were strangling him.

'Well, sit down then,' Dorothy said, and he obeyed, sitting on the very edge of a chair, hitching up his trouser legs, and speaking in a low voice as if he were in chapel.

'Did you tell them I was coming?'

Dorothy sat down opposite to him on the massive chester-field, curling her legs up beneath her. 'Well, I daren't after what you said this afternoon, dare I? But in any case, Gerald was here, and I went up to my room.' Her eyes clouded. 'Honestly, he gives me the willies. I know I won't be able to talk naturally to him till this thing's sorted out. I've got a feeling he knows I suspect something.' She twisted a strand of hair round her finger. 'He's like a slimy snake, except that snakes are really dry.'

Stanley stared at the cut-glass sherry decanter on the low table by the side of his chair, flanked by four glasses arranged in pairs. Just for a moment he forgot the seriousness of what he had come for as he thought of the contrast between those sparkling glasses and the amber-coloured liquid, and the mugs of stout he guessed his mother would be drinking with Nellie Crawley.

'You haven't said anything to your mother and father? You kept it to yourself like I said?'

Dorothy narrowed blue eyes at him. 'I daren't say a word about anything, I told you. I'm scared of you, you were so fierce this afternoon. No, I'll keep it to myself for the time being,' she said calmly. 'I had a long think about what you said, and you're right. I'm too impulsive, always have been, and he's not likely to run away, is he? Not when he's decided to brazen it out.'

'Aw, Dorothy.' Stanley's tone was rueful. 'All right then, just suppose there is something in what you say? No, he won't run away, just as long as he doesn't suspect that we suspect.'

'We? I thought you rejected everything I said? That's how it seemed to me this afternoon.'

Stanley's thin face took on what she thought of as his suffering look. Its holier-than-thou look, she thought with a twinge of irritation. Funny how different he looked sitting there in her own familiar surroundings. Uncomfortable, wary, frightened almost. As if he were perched there on the edge of the chair ready to get up and run from the room at any given moment. Poised for flight. Out of place. He didn't match, she thought sadly. Everything else in the room matched, but Stanley Armstrong didn't. Suddenly she felt scared.

'Come over and sit next to me,' she invited, patting the

moquette cover with her hand. 'It's quite safe, they'll not be back for ages yet.'

And then, as he took her in his arms and held her close, as his lips searched for hers and closed over them with the familiar hard closed-mouth kiss, it was all right again.

'Oh, Dorothy, you're so beautiful, you're the most beautiful girl in the world,' he whispered. Then he kissed her again, and this time the kiss was deeper, and as they clung together she could feel his heart thudding like a sledge-hammer against his ribs. How thin he was! She ran her hands over his shoulders. And how young he was, how very young! And vulnerable. She held him closer still and felt him tremble.

This wasn't the same as kissing in the park, or on the back row of the pictures, or in a darkened shop doorway. Then she hadn't experienced this overwhelming sense of power, this knowing that in spite of his cleverness, his practical theories, she was the one in charge. It was wonderful and it was terrible. Terrible and sort of disappointing. She buried her head in his green woollen chest and caught the unmistakable whiff of moth-balls. How awful if she started to giggle! So far she was quite unmoved. Pleasured, but quite unmoved. She stretched her body out on the wide cushions and felt his body adapt itself to hers. Felt his chest, his loins, and a hardness that made her catch her breath with surprise.

His face was hot against her own, burning as if he had a fever. She made no move to stop him when his hand fumbled with the buttons of her blouse, caught her breath again then as she felt the feather-light touch of his fingers on her nipples, she felt them grow hard and whimpered as the heat rose in her own body.

'Oh, Dorothy,' he moaned, and she tangled her fingers in the springiness of his hair, and pulled his head down, and as his mouth closed over her breast, she jerked her head back with a low sound of delight.

Then, with a suddenness that left her limp and disbelieving, he sat up away from her, pulled the front of her blouse together, and in a voice that shook, begged her to forgive him.

'I'm sorry,' he muttered, looking away from her into the fire. 'I shouldn't have done that. Can you ever forgive me?'

Buttoning up her blouse, Dorothy refused to look at him.

'I respect you,' he insisted.

'I know you do,' she comforted.

Then he covered his face with his hands and groaned aloud.

What he could never tell her was that he might have gone further, might even have tried to . . . but that even as he caressed her he had suddenly been reminded of what had happened to Ruby. In another moment his self-control might have snapped and then he would have been no better, tarred with the same brush as that man, that unknown man who had forced himself on his sister and taken away her virginity. For she had been a virgin until then, just as Dorothy was a virgin. He knew it, and the knowledge of what he might have done filled him with a revulsion against his own sex.

'I'll never spoil thee, Dorothy,' he said quietly, using the Lancashire dialect as he always did when moved.

Dorothy got up and going over to the mantelpiece, took down a silver cigarette box. Her face was flushed and her eyes as heavy as if she'd been crying. He thought she had never looked lovelier.

She held the box out to him. 'Have a smoke. Go on, I can wash the ashtray before they come back.'

He stretched out his hand to the neatly layered cigarettes, marvelling at the length, their firmness. Already he could feel the tang of the smoke curling round his tongue, the steadying of his nerves as he inhaled. 'They'll smell it, won't they?' he said.

'The whole house reeks of my father's pipe, hadn't you noticed? My mother's tried everything, from a cut onion in a saucer to spraying the air with her precious lavender water.' Then as he took one she placed a heavy cut-glass ashtray on the little table by his side.

'I've decided to let Beryl in on it,' she said.

He stopped in the act of lighting up. 'Beryl?' he repeated, his face a study in disbelief.

Dorothy sighed. 'My cousin down the road. You know. I told you this afternoon. I told you that Gerald had sworn her to secrecy about losing the cuff-links, remember? He wants her on his side too. In case any awkward questions are asked, don't you see?' She took the spent match from his fingers and threw it impatiently into the fire. 'Don't look so . . . so affronted! We won't mention your Ruby, we'll just say that we suspect that Gerald is being unfaithful to Margaret, and we want her to help us to catch him out. She's so romantic that if she thinks it's all in the cause of true love, or untrue love, she'll do anything she can to help. After Gerald confiding in her, then us, she'll feel like a double agent, can't you see? So when you've finished that cigarette we'll go down to her house. It's only down the road, and I know she's in on her own because her mother and father have gone out with my parents, to the same place. Yes, that's what we'll do. We'll talk to Beryl, then we'll have a dekko in Gerald's room.'

'Now look, Dorothy.' Stanley shook his head from side to side as if he couldn't believe that the girl planning and scheming so coolly could possibly be the same girl who, not five minutes before, had lain in his arms, as carried away as he had been. He could have sworn it. Now she was tapping with her foot on the floor, waiting for him to pull himself together and finish his cigarette. He was learning about women, he was, aye by heck, he was learning fast.

He saw that his hand still trembled as he held the cigarette to his lips, and scorned his own weakness. 'Now look, Dorothy,' he said more firmly. 'I've been thinking about what you said ever since you said it, and there's nothing – not one shred of evidence that would stand up in any court in the land. I don't know what's come over you, and that's a fact.' He drew deeply on the cigarette. 'He couldn't have been meeting our Ruby on the sly and not told the police when this happened. He'd be bound to know they'll find out. Somebody would have seen them together. Somebody always does. Look how many people have told your mother about seeing *us*.'

'He has a car,' Dorothy said slowly, emphasizing each word as if she were talking to a backward five-year-old. 'And it was the winter when he was meeting Ruby, remember? Dark, Stanley Armstrong. Dark.'

She sat down and clasped her hands round her knees. 'All right then, maybe I did get carried away this afternoon, but he *knew* her, Stanley. I've seen his eyes when it's come up, and oh, he knew her all right. And if he knew her and had been seeing her then he could perhaps help the police to find out who murdered her.' She lifted a knee with her clasped hands and rocked herself backwards and forwards. 'Oh, my God, I feel it so strongly, can't you see? I've never hated anyone in my life before, but I hate Gerald Tomlin so much I can actually feel my skin crawl when he's near to me. Do you believe in spiritual perception, Stanley?'

'Perception yes, but not necessarily spiritual.'

'Well then. He's scared half out of his wits, Stanley. He is. Honestly. And next month he's going to marry my sister, who is about as perceptive as that standard lamp over there, and that doesn't mean I don't love her dearly because I do. And if you won't come with me to Beryl's, then I'll go myself, and you can go home.'

'Dorothy! Stop it. I don't know you when you're like this.' His voice was filled with reproach.

She held her head high. 'You know me a bit better after tonight though, don't you, Stanley Armstrong?'

'Come here,' he said softly, crushing the cigarette out in the ashtray. 'I promise I'll be good this time.' Then as he wrapped her in his arms, he whispered into her hair. 'I need you so much. I just want to hold you like this, and close my eyes and pretend nothing awful has happened. I want to pretend this is our house, and you are my wife, and I want to forget I've left me mum crying by the fire waiting till Monday when they'll be burying our Ruby on top of me dad in the cemetery.' He stroked her cheek gently. 'There's so much that's good in the world, Dorothy, so much of it right here in this room, and I want a part of it . . . I'm selfish and cruel because I don't want to go back down the hill to Inkerman Street. I'm dreading Monday, and having to be brave for me mum's sake. I want it all to go away, Dorothy. I want to pretend just for a little while that it never happened. You don't know how awful it is in that house. I feel I'm breathing now for the first time since it happened.'

She held his hand to her cheek and turned her lips to it, then froze into instant watchful silence as she heard the grating of a key in the lock of the big front door.

'Oh, my God, they've come back! Pretend you've come about the funeral. Just act normal. They can't *do* anything.'

She was moving with the speed of light, emptying the ashtray into the fire, tucking her blouse into her skirt, moving to sit as far away from him as she could, so that when the door opened they were sitting there stiffly as if arranged, like dummies in a shop window.

And it wasn't, as she had thought it would be, her mother and father returning early from their bridge party, but Margaret, radiant with happiness, followed into the room by Gerald Tomlin.

Thirteen

'Well? What did I tell you?' Dorothy said as soon as the big front door closed behind them. She was pulling at Stanley's hand urging him on, and he felt he'd had enough, more than enough. His mind, still dazed with grief, his *academic* mind, geared to study, to the assimilation of facts, to the light relief of what he realized now had been merely surface conversations with the girl at his side, reeled dizzily from what had just happened.

He hardly recognized the determined set of Dorothy's face, saw nothing of the former quiet acceptance of her devotion. She was *obsessed*, he told himself, totally obsessed.

'Did you see the way his face changed when he saw you?' she demanded. 'What did you think about him? Don't you think his eyes are strange? Could you even bear to look at them knowing . . . ?'

'We know nothing,' Stanley said. 'You must be crazy. Do you realize what you're saying?' He shook his head wearily from side to side. 'Folks have been hung for less.'

He took her by the elbows and forced her to stand still. 'Give me a chance to think, to *breathe* for heaven's sake.' She was dancing with impatience, but still he held her fast. 'Dorothy. Dorothy. Calm down, please. What they must think of us rushing out like that, I don't know. You should have stayed and let me talk to him, given me a chance to weigh him up. I felt a fool, an utter fool.' He looked back over his shoulder to the house. 'I should have stood my ground, not allowed you to rush me out of the room; they're probably laughing their heads off at us now. And if there is anything in what you say, if he did know Ruby, then by our very behaviour he's bound to know that we suspect.'

A man walking his dog went by and glanced at them with curiosity, and Stanley waited until he was well out of ear-shot.

'And as for saying that Gerald's face changed, well, of course it changed. He came into that room and saw us sitting there, both looking as guilty as hell, then without a hallo or a goodbye, you grab me by the hand and drag me out of the room, as if I were a naughty child, snatching up our coats in the hall and banging the front door behind us. Of course his face changed. He'll think we're mad, completely out of our minds. That's what he'll think and that's all.'

Dorothy wriggled impatiently out of his grasp and started to walk quickly ahead of him, so that even with his long loping stride he had difficulty in keeping up with her. She talked furiously to him over her shoulder.

'Gerald Tomlin *knew* who you were. There was no need to say anything, because he knew.' She pulled savagely at a privet hedge, then scattered the leaves on the ground as if leaving a paper-chase for Stanley to follow. 'He knew who you were because you look like your sister. You told me how alike you were.' Her voice rang with triumph. 'If he hadn't known that I was friendly with you, he would have known who you were. And it was a shock. A terrible shock. I saw his face go white. His face went white and those funny wet eyes of his dilated; I wouldn't have been surprised if he'd dropped down on the floor in a dead faint.'

She turned into the wide driveway of a detached house, the gates and the garage door left open for a returning car. 'This is where my cousin Beryl lives. You can come in with me, Stanley, or you can go home. You can go back down Inkerman Street, and you can tell your mother that you've met the man who I believe got your Ruby into trouble, even if he didn't kill her. You can tell her that and you can say that you quite liked the look of him, actually.'

'Dorothy!' Stanley's voice was more of a groan. 'What did you expect me to do, then? Knock him down when I can't think of a single reason for doing so? Dorothy. Please listen to me. I'm listening to *you*, honestly I am. I'm listening and I'm thinking, and as soon as you tell me one single fact that makes me even slightly suspicious, then I'll tell the police, whether he's your future brother-in-law, or not. But it's dangerous talk. Can't you see? Do you ever stop to think that you could be turning your dislike of Gerald into a reason for all this wild talk? Do you mean that you expected me to accuse him, then and there?'

As Dorothy put her finger on the door-bell, a chime of bells ding-donged up and down the scale, and Stanley leant against the door-post, feeling in need of its solid support.

Dorothy pressed the bell again. 'Surely Beryl's not in bed at this time? She's probably been told not to answer the door. I'll shout through the letter-box if she doesn't come in a minute.'

Stanley kicked at a loose piece of gravel. 'I suppose they'll tell your mother and father that I was there? I'd much rather have come openly the first time and met them properly, like a civilized being.'

Just for a fleeting moment Dorothy was caught off guard. The thought that her mother did not regard this tall troubled boy as a civilized being flashed through her mind. His mother took in washing, and his sister worked in a cotton mill and had been ill-bred enough to get herself pregnant, and murdered. And yet his code of honour, his innate sense of what was right and proper was far greater than her own . . . There was something wrong somewhere.

'They won't tell,' she said, 'that's the last thing they'll do. Sisters don't sneak on each other, and Gerald certainly won't mention meeting you.'

'Seeing me, not meeting me.'

'Well, seeing you then. Oh no, Gerald won't want to start a discussion about you or anything to do with you. He can't

145

bear your family to be mentioned, Margaret told me. Something to do with his sensitive disposition. He makes me sick. Can't you see?'

'There's someone coming,' Stanley said miserably. He felt ill, and the hammering in his head was starting up again. The tension of the past few days was taking its inevitable toll, and the cool logic he prided himself on was deserting him with every passing minute. He was behaving totally out of character, and Dorothy had changed out of all recognition from the girl he thought he knew. The Dorothy he knew had been content to listen to his views for hours at a time, her pretty face aglow with admiration as he expounded his views on life in general, and Stanley Armstrong and his ambitions in particular.

Ruby was dead, gone for ever, and something in him had died with her. What had happened to her that night in the park so filled his mind with animal loathing that in some strange inexplicable way he had transferred some of that emotion to the girl now tapping her foot impatiently as she waited for the door to open. And if he had done what he'd wanted to do he would have been no better than that unknown man who had squeezed Ruby's breath out of her, then left her with her black hair tangled with mud and leaves. The enormity of what had almost happened caught at his own throat as surely as if fingers pressed on his windpipe.

And all he really wanted to do was to mourn. To scream and yell his grief aloud; to stop trying to be a man with a stiff upper lip, as stiff as the collars his mother dipped into her bowl of starch. All he wanted to do was to put his head down somewhere and cleanse himself with tears.

But somebody was calling out from the other side of the big ornate front door.

'Yes? Who is it, please?'

Dorothy raised exasperated blue eyes skywards. 'It's Dorothy. Open the door, Beryl. It's not Jack the Ripper.'

And if Cousin Beryl had not been already tucked up in

146

bed, it was obvious that she was on her way there. The dark brown woollen dressing-gown, its cord pulled tightly round her thick waist, did less than nothing for her sallow complexion, and the side pieces of her lank brown hair were rolled up in steel curlers. As she saw Stanley standing beside Dorothy, her hands went straight to them, pulling at them in an attempt to wrench them out. Two spots, chalky with calamine lotion, disfigured her rounded chin.

'Oh, Dorothy.' Her eyebrows were sending a message to her cousin, and Stanley read it correctly.

'How could you come and bring him without letting me know? Now he's seen me looking like this, and I'll feel awful every time I see him.'

Once, a long time ago, he had let Eddie Marsden in when Ruby was sitting by the fire with a towel round her newly washed hair, and she had given him what for afterwards. 'You could have left him on the door-step till I'd had time to run upstairs,' she'd stormed. And Ruby had been exactly the same age as this fat girl, stiff with embarrassment, dithering in the porch, tearing at the steel curlers in her hair.

'You'd better come in then,' she said ungraciously, and miserably Stanley stepped behind Dorothy into a square hall, an almost exact replica of the one he'd recently stepped out of, apart from the fact that the walls were papered in a bottle-green geometric design instead of being wood-panelled.

'You know Stanley by sight, don't you?' Dorothy made the introduction casually, walking before them into the room on the right and leaving Stanley shaking hands with a totally demoralized Beryl who was trying to wipe off the calamine lotion and take out the one remaining curler at the same time.

'I'm sorry,' he whispered, meaning it even as he realized how stupid it sounded.

'And I'm sorry about . . .' Beryl said, blushing so red that her eyes seemed to sparkle with unshed tears.

147

'It's all right,' Stanley said inadequately.

They walked into a large room papered with a design as glumly oppressive as that in the hall. In spite of his misery Stanley looked around him with curiosity, and his mind registered the fact that never in his life had he seen so ugly a room. The cosy little living-room at home with its black fireplace and the firelight flickering on the cream distempered walls seemed almost luxurious by comparison. Here the paper-frieze, following the lines of the picture-rail, was a design of bright yellow hanging blossoms, and the doors and window-frames were painted in an only slightly subdued shade of the same colour. The vast tiled fireplace had a ziggurat motif which was faithfully reflected in the carpet, and the chairs and sofa were upholstered in cold, unyielding leather.

'Sit down then,' Beryl told him, and smiled for the first time.

She sat down opposite to him and fixed an unwinking gaze on him.

'Have you been to the pictures?' Her hand flew to her mouth, like a naughty child caught out saying something she shouldn't. 'Oh, golly, I'm sorry. Of course you won't have been to the pictures, not with . . . with everything. Oh, gosh.'

'It's all right,' Stanley said again.

Dorothy stood between them, her hands in her blazer pocket. 'Beryl? Can we trust you?'

Stanley winced. 'Look, I don't really think . . .'

'Can we, Beryl?'

The round brown eyes almost popped out with the vehemence of Beryl's nod.

'Cut my throat and hope to die.'

'We want more than that.' Dorothy walked purposefully over to a glass-fronted bookcase and opening the door with a small key already in the lock, took out a large, leather-bound Bible. 'Right, now come over here, Beryl.'

Stanley wished himself anywhere but where he was. He

wished he had stayed at home. He wished he was dead. . . .

Dorothy opened the Bible with a flourish, and put it down on a chromium and glass-topped table. 'Place your hand there then.'

And obeying at once, striped pyjama legs flapping beneath the boy's-style dressing-gown, Beryl walked over to her cousin and laid a podgy hand on the open page.

'I swear to keep my mouth shut about what I am about to hear. For the time being,' Dorothy prompted.

'I swear to keep my mouth shut. For the time being,' Beryl repeated in tones of awe.

'Right.' Dorothy slammed the Bible shut and returned it to its place in the bookcase. 'Now listen. We've found out . . .' She glanced briefly in Stanley's direction and sighed. 'At least, we *think* we've found out that Gerald Tomlin is being unfaithful to Margaret.' She refused to look at Stanley. 'We think he may even have got a girl into trouble, and we want you to help us to prove it.'

'But they're getting married . . .' Beryl sat down with an ungainly thump on the nearest brown leather chair. 'Oh, how awful! I can't believe it. They're madly in love. Passionately,' she added, blushing again in deference to Stanley's presence.

'Maybe. That's as maybe,' Dorothy said, 'and we think there may be evidence, proof, rather, in his bedroom.' She turned her back on Stanley. 'So I'm going up there to have a look round, and you're going to stay down here with Stanley, and on my way up I'm going to bolt the door, so that should anyone come back, they won't be able to get in, and I'll have time to get back downstairs.'

Beryl looked as if she might be going to burst into tears. 'And what will I say then if they do come back? What will I tell my mother when she asks why the door was bolted? That's what I want to know.'

Dorothy glanced at Stanley for sympathy, and found none.

'You'll think of something. Anyway, if they do come back

149

they'll be more concerned about you having a boy in the house than about the door being bolted. And you can blame that on me.'

Beryl took a large handkerchief from her pocket and screwed it up into a ball. 'It's all right for you, Dorothy Bolton. I'll be the one who gets into trouble, not you. My mother will kill me if she finds out. She made me promise not to open the door to anyone.'

'Gerald excepted of course.' Dorothy was already on her way to the door. 'Oh, the irony of it.'

'I'm coming with you,' Stanley stood up, not knowing, as Mrs Crawley would have said, whether he was bloody coming or bloody going.

'No, you stay here with Beryl, then if I get found out you won't be involved. I won't be long.'

And Dorothy disappeared; they heard her running light-footed up the stairs.

Stanley and Beryl stared at each other, transfixed.

'My mother would kill me,' Beryl said. 'I'm not brave like Dorothy. She – my mother I mean – she stopped me playing with Dorothy when we were little girls because she was always getting me into trouble.' She started to fringe the end of her dressing-gown cord. 'She thinks it's awful, Auntie Phyllis – that's Dorothy's mother – allowing Dorothy to go out with you.' She was far too upset to weigh her words. 'And if she knew that you'd both been in here whilst they were out, she'd blame me.' She bit her lip. 'And as for her going up to Gerald's room. Oh, it's awful. I've looked in the doorway many a time, but I've never been in. My conscience wouldn't let me.'

'She's thinking about her sister's happiness,' Stanley said with some desperation, feeling loyalty of some kind was called for.

Footsteps walked up and down on the other side of the high ceiling, and for a moment it seemed that the big glass light fitting shivered. Stanley shivered with it. Since Dorothy had left the room her cousin's raisin brown eyes

150

had never left his face.

'She stares at Gerald,' he remembered Dorothy saying, and for a moment felt a twinge of sympathy.

'Dorothy's got this bee in her bonnet,' he said. 'I think I'll go up and fetch her down. You're right, Beryl, it's not fair to you.'

'No!' Her voice rang with the beginnings of hysteria. 'Oh, it's awful! If anyone was to come back, and you were upstairs with Dorothy, they'd think you were . . .' She closed her eyes in horror. 'They'd think you were . . . well, upstairs and everything, both of you, and me downstairs.' Her voice tailed off as she blushed scarlet, overcome with an embarrassment she would live through for days just remembering. 'My mother's very strict with me. She doesn't allow me to go out with boys. Oh gosh!' She plucked at the dressing-gown cord with frantic fingers. Now what had she gone and said? This boy's sister, sixteen like herself, had been allowed to go out with boys, had actually done *it*. Oh, gosh, how awful! It wasn't his fault. He was nice, far too nice for her bossy cousin rooting around in Gerald's room upstairs. She stared at him straight in the eye.

'What's your favourite subject at school, Stanley?' she asked with a kindly but stunned kind of desperation.

Dorothy found what she was looking for within minutes of entering Gerald's room. On top of the walnut tall-boy was a round leather stud-box, and inside was an assortment of studs and cuff-links. She took it over to the bed and turned it upside down on the quilted satin bedspread. The back-studs she pushed aside and concentrated on sorting out the cuff-links. Eight pairs in all, including the pair she had seen Gerald wearing the night of the Police Ball, the second bigger pair he had bought secretly at Adamson's the jewellers.

With one link spare. The slightly smaller type she had seen Margaret buy as an engagement present weeks before.

151

Her heart-beat quickened as she tossed it from one hand to the other. So she was right. He had come in that terrible night with one link missing, and in his agitation had not know where he had lost it, had even dared to hope that he had dropped it in his room as he tore frantically at his clothes before getting into bed and burying his face in the pillow to shut out the sound of Ruby's dying gasps. Her imagination soared. Then, with the cuff-link in her hand, she got up from the bed and began to pace the room. Backwards and forwards, forwards and backwards, taking in the contents of the room with the surface of her mind.

The blue silk dressing-gown hanging in disciplined folds from a hook behind the door, the tortoise-shell brushes laid out side by side on the dressing-table with its three mirrors reflecting her worried face in triplicate. The row of books on the shelf behind the bed. Auntie Ethel's hideous taste in furnishings, the olive-green of the bedspread at shiny shouting variance with the electric-blue curtains hanging at the tall windows. And the all pervading smell of Gerald's lavender-scented brilliantine. She wrinkled her nose in distaste.

Then suddenly the sound of a car, the revving of an engine pulled her up sharp. Gerald was coming back! Frantically, as she shuffled the studs and cuff-links back into the leather box, she tried to remember if the red sports car had been in the garage as she came up the drive with Stanley. Had she seen it, or had she been too preoccupied with trying to make Beryl answer the door that she hadn't noticed? Pulling the door behind her she flew down the stairs, and went into the sitting-room where two pairs of startled eyebrows raised themselves in urgent enquiry.

'I thought I heard Gerald's car,' she said, but Beryl shook her head. 'It's in the garage. He left it there and walked to your house with Margaret. I watched them from the landing window.'

Dorothy collapsed rather than sat down in the nearest chair. 'My God, but it was spooky up there. I thought I'd have heart failure when I heard that car.' Her laugh had more than a touch of hysteria in it. 'I was out of that room quicker than a drink of water.'

Stanley stood up. 'Well, I hope you're satisfied. What you hoped to find I don't know, but I'm going home. Right now, Dorothy.' He turned to Beryl. 'You've been a sport.' Doubling his hand into a fist he touched her lightly on the shoulder. 'Now you'll know me the next time you see me.'

'I won't tell,' Beryl said, her face as solemn and her eyes as round as a night owl's.

'She won't, you know,' Dorothy said in the hall, bending down and unbolting the front door.

'She's a good kid,' Stanley said. 'Come on, I'll see you home.'

Dorothy shook her head. 'I'll just go back and have another word with Beryl.'

'Then I'll wait for you.'

'No, there's no need, honestly. It's only a hop skip and jump.' His face in the darkness was tense-looking and sad, and she laid her cheek briefly against the sleeve of the shabby jacket.

'Don't look so worried, please, Stanley. I won't do anything stupid, honestly. And Beryl won't say anything. I know her, she'll think it's all too romantic for words.'

'What? About Gerald being what you said he was?'

'No, about meeting you, I mean.'

'And Gerald?'

She turned her face into his shoulder so that her voice came muffled, 'Oh, forget that for now. I was so scared up there in his room I don't want to think about it . . . you'd best go now. And Stanley?'

'Hmm?'

'I'll be thinking about you on Monday. I'll be at school, but I'll be thinking about you every single minute.'

Suddenly she wanted to put her arms round him and cry and cry, and the feeling was as overwhelming as the fear that had caught her by the throat in the upstairs room not five minutes before. 'Go now. And God bless.'

She didn't ever remember saying that before. It was what the vicar always said when they took their leave of him in the church porch every Sunday morning. It was what her father used to say when he tucked her up in bed when she was a child and she would have no one but him to bid her good night. And it was what Grandpa Bolton had always said. 'God bless, lovey. God bless.'

Then Stanley walked away from her, and she watched him go as she always seemed to be watching him go. Head bent, with the long, loping careless stride, wrists protruding from the awful jacket. Sighing, she went back into the sitting-room.

Beryl was standing in front of a large bean-shaped mirror, busy with the curlers again.

'You might have rung up and said you were bringing Stanley round,' she grumbled, licking her thumb and forefinger and sliding a piece of hair between them. 'How do you think I felt with him seeing me in my dressing-gown and with my hair all pinned up?' Her eyes were suddenly sly. 'You'd been snogging, hadn't you? I can see a love-bite on your neck. He's nice, and I felt ever so sorry for him. He didn't like you going up to Gerald's room one little bit. He didn't say anything, but I knew. And anyway, what does it matter if Gerald has been unfaithful to your Margaret? Men always have a past, and it will be awful if you go and spoil the wedding now. And if some silly girl has got herself into trouble then it's her fault. It's always the girl who eggs the boy on; a boy gets worked up quicker than a girl. And anyway, it's only that sort of girl who gets worked up anyway.'

Dorothy closed her eyes. 'You've sworn on the Holy Bible not to tell, remember?'

'I know, and I'll be damned to eternal hell-fire if I tell. I *know*. That's two secrets I'm keeping now. I wish I had one of my jolly own to keep.' She rubbed her stomach. 'I think I'll go and have a biscuit.'

'And I'm going.' Dorothy hesitated. 'Do you *like* Gerald, Beryl? As a person I mean?'

Beryl was already en route for the biscuit barrel. 'I've never really thought about it. He's a bit of a dark horse, I suppose.'

'How is he a dark horse?'

Beryl pulled at her bottom lip. 'Well, like I told you, before he fell in love with your Margaret, he used to go off in his car and just say he was going out. That was a bit rude, wasn't it?'

'Unless he had something to hide?'

Dorothy followed her cousin into the kitchen, and shook her head when the biscuit barrel was held out to her.

'I'll tell you one thing.' Beryl spoke through a mouthful of Marie biscuit. 'We had a policeman round just before tea.'

Dorothy held her breath. 'Go on.'

Beryl took another biscuit. 'Well, you know they're asking all the men in the whole town where they were on the night Stanley's sister was killed.'

'Yes, I know.'

'Gosh, I'm hungry. Well, when they went to the mill Gerald was out, so they came here. They were coming here, anyway, to ask my father. He was at the Masons.'

'And Gerald?' The clock was ticking so loudly that Dorothy glanced towards it. 'And *Gerald*?'

'Well, he said that he'd gone for one of his drives in his car. You know, I told you, he was always going for drives.'

'Yes. Yes?'

'I'll just have one more biscuit. Well, he said he had been for a drive that night, but he hadn't. He went out, but he didn't take his car. He walked.'

'How do you know?'

'Because I watched him from the landing window. He left the car in the garage that night.'

Dorothy sat down on a kitchen chair.

'And you told the police that?'

155

Beryl sniffed. 'As if I would. He only forgot, didn't he? As if everybody will remember exactly what they were doing that night, and anyway, I would have to have said I was watching, wouldn't I? And Gerald would have known I watch him, wouldn't he? And he would have got cross, and I don't like him being cross, do I?'

She reluctantly placed the lid on the biscuit barrel. 'Anyway, what does it matter whether he went out in the car or walked? He had nothing to do with that horrible murder, had he?'

'Of course he hadn't.' Dorothy spoke quickly. 'So he's been cross with you before, has he, Beryl?'

But even as she opened her mouth to answer, there was the sound of a key grating in the lock, and for the second time that night Dorothy froze.

'He's back. I'm going. Out the back way. Better he doesn't know I've been here. All right?'

'It's all right, he's going straight upstairs, he often does that. He doesn't have any supper.' Beryl's voice was hoarse with biscuit crumbs.

But putting her finger to her lips, Dorothy turned the key in the back door and slipped outside, leaving Beryl with her own finger to her lips in rather mystified understanding.

'See you at church tomorrow.'

'Suppose so.'

Then she was outside in the narrow passage-way between the house and the garage, outside in the road, running, with her heart pounding and her thoughts so chaotic that her mind was a formless blank.

And it wasn't until she was walking up her own drive that Dorothy put her hand in her blazer pocket and felt the cuff-link, hard and round . . . and the knowledge that she had, in her headlong flight from Gerald's room forgotten to replace it, filled her with terror.

If she was right. If there was anything in what she suspected, then her safe little world was safe no longer.

From now on Gerald Tomlin would know that someone knew. And knowing would turn him from a merely frightened man to a man of desperation.

Fourteen

Before Dorothy had closed the door behind her, even before she had gone swiftly upstairs, knowing she could not, at that moment, face Margaret, she had decided what to do with the cuff-link, weighing now as heavy as lead in her blazer pocket.

She would have to take a chance on Gerald discovering its loss that night, and the next morning, in church, she would pass it over to Beryl, saying she had slipped it in her pocket, accidentally, when she thought she'd heard Gerald's car outside, reminding the luckless Beryl of her sworn promise and the threat of hell-fire if she went back on it.

And if Beryl refused she would go back with her cousin to the house and somehow, some way, she would put it back herself.

Of one thing she was absolutely certain. The cuff-link had to be replaced. Because, in a strange paradoxical way, now that she held what could have been evidence of Gerald's involvement in her hand, she was convinced of his innocence.

Thinking he was guilty was one thing; actually proving it, she was finding already, was another.

And if Gerald was a typical man, if he was anything like her own father, he would wriggle out of the shirt he had been wearing that day with the links still in place. How often had she heard her mother reprimanding her father for doing just that?

'One of these days, Matthew, Mrs Wilkinson will put them out still fastened to your shirt for the laundry-man, and that will be that. Surely it's only a small thing to ask. Quite honestly I don't understand you, Matthew.'

But Gerald didn't have a wife who nagged. Not yet. Gerald Tomlin might not be a murderer, but he was the kind of man to whom neatness and order were the equivalent of a second skin. The kind of man who would pull his shirt over his shiny red head, sit down on the shiny bedspread in that meticulously tidy room, then take the cuff-links out of his cuffs and put them in the leather box on the tall-boy.

Dorothy tiptoed across the landing, and closing her bedroom door behind her, leant against it, shutting her eyes as if she would shut out the terrifying supposition. For if he found the odd one missing when he lifted the round lid, if he checked . . . oh dear God, what would he do? Especially if there was any truth in what she had been convincing herself was not the truth? Her vivid imagination soared on black wings, into a nightmare situation where the smooth-tongued Gerald, smooth-tongued no longer, confronted a quaking Beryl, forcing her to admit that she had been in his room.

'I swear I haven't,' Beryl would say, shaking with terror inside the brown woollen dressing-gown.'

And Gerald would think that the police had been, searching his room, searching for the cuff-link that was the twin to the one they had found buried by leaves beside Ruby's dead body.

Now Dorothy's imagination had run away with her, completely and terrifyingly out of even a semblance of control. How could she have thought a moment ago that Gerald was innocent?

'I tell you, Gerald. I swear that no one has been in your room. How could they have been when I've been alone all evening?'

That was Beryl, thinking of the hell-fire awaiting her if she broke her vow of silence.

'The truth, or I'll . . . or I'll . . .'

That was Gerald Tomlin, narrow-set eyes blazing, who having killed once, had nothing to lose.

His hands, those sinewy hands, with the ginger hairs sprouting sickeningly from between his knuckles, were reaching out for Beryl's plump throat. Her poor, silly little cousin, whose death would lie irrevocably at Dorothy's door. . . .

Dorothy screamed aloud as the door was pushed open, sending her almost sprawling on the carpet. Beryl had proved no heroine and Gerald was here, to demand an explanation! Dorothy felt the hair on her head gently raise itself away from her crawling scalp.

'For goodness sakes! It's only me. What on earth's the matter with you, Dorothy? First you rush out of the house, dragging that poor boy with you, and now you behave as though I've just walked in with my head tucked underneath my arm.'

Margaret was smiling, very much the elder sister, teasing, patronizing, serene in her own cocoon of happiness, generously tolerant because of it. Her golden hair was sweetly disarranged, and at the corner of her smiling mouth her plum coloured lipstick was tellingly smudged. She walked over to the dressing-table and smiled at her reflection, well pleased with herself, and spoke soothingly over her shoulder.

'I'm not going to split on you, our Dorothy. Surely you don't think for one moment that I would? It's not a crime having a boy in when Mother and Father go out.' She went pink. 'Though I do hope you know what you're doing. Some boys would take advantage, you know. They're not all as nice as Gerald, or as your Stanley. I wouldn't have minded having a chat with him, the poor boy, shown him how sorry we all are. He must be going through a dreadful time just now.'

Dorothy said nothing. Her heart was still pounding as, carefully wriggling both arms out of the blazer sleeve, she took it off, holding it straight in case the cuff-link did the unthinkable and rolled out of the pocket and on to the floor. Then, with measured movements, she took a hanger from her wardrobe and put the coat away, closing the door, and turning the key in the lock.

'What did you say?' she asked.

Margaret twisted round on the dressing-table stool, still smiling.

'Oh, never mind. But there's no need for you to be in such a tiz-woz, honestly, love. We won't talk about it if you don't want to.' She put her head on one side and spoke slowly, like a kindergarten teacher calming down a naughty child. 'Now then. Tomorrow morning after church, Gerald and I are going over to the house to do some measuring in the kitchen. Why don't you come with us? We can help Mother with the vegetables for the dinner before we go if we get up early enough.'

Dorothy sat down on the bed, and stared at the pointed toes of her black court shoes. 'Is Gerald going to church with us then? I thought he was a non-believer?'

Margaret frowned. 'Well, actually, he's meeting me outside with the car, but he did go when the banns were being read, remember? And it isn't that he doesn't believe really, you know. It's just that organized religion doesn't appeal to him. He thinks that one can be as close to God in the middle of a field, or out on the moors.'

'Or in the park?' Dorothy heard herself say.

'Well, yes, in the park if you wish.' Margaret leaned forward, clasping her hands earnestly between her knees. 'Look, Dorothy. That mention of the park came right up out of your subconscious, didn't it? I've been reading a book about that sort of thing. From the library. You'll have to try to forget that terrible happening in the park, you know.'

'How?' Dorothy glanced towards the wardrobe door, then quickly away again.

Margaret shook her head, more in sorrow than anger. 'I

know it must be difficult you being so friendly with that poor girl's brother and everything. But terrible things do happen in life, and if we took them all to heart, then we'd never know a single moment's peace.' She looked lovingly at Dorothy sitting with shoulders hunched almost up to her ears. Genuine sympathy filled her heart and her voice, and even as she went on she heard herself modulating her voice in deference to her sister's sadness. 'You're sensitive, like me. We're a sensitive family. All the Boltons are sensitive. Even Father, though he does appear to be a bit gruff and outspoken on the surface.'

Dorothy lifted her head for a moment and stared at her sister in surprise. 'But Father is the most sensitive of us all,' she wanted to say, then saw it was no use. Margaret was blinking her eyes as if trying to remember a verse from a poem to illustrate her meaning. '*Oh, God, please let her get up and go, and let her not read the evil thoughts that beset me,*' she prayed silently, but Margaret was obviously determined to have her well-intentioned say.

'I've never told you this before, Dorothy, but reading that library book showed me how wrong it is to dwell on the sordid.' She put up a finger and stroked a smooth cheek. 'And, anyway, you get wrinkles if you think negative thoughts for any length of time. But once, a long time ago, when I was about seven years old, a girl who was in the same Brownie Pack as me died of diphtheria. She was called Elsie. Or was it Enid? No, it was definitely Elsie. Well, although Mother would have had a pink fit, me and another girl went to the house and took a bunch of flowers, and for some reason Elsie's mother asked us in and took us into the parlour where the coffin was.' Margaret's placid face grew crumpled lines with the effort of making herself clear. 'She, the dead girl, was dressed in her Brownie uniform, with her Pixie badge sewn above the pocket, and all the badges she'd earned sewn down her sleeve. There was a great big mirror on the wall, and the whole terrible thing was reflected in it. There were two little curtains pulled to over her face, but her hands were white and crossed over her chest, and the coffin was flanked by two huge vases of carnations. It was awful. Can you imagine? The smell was something I'll never forget, sort of sickly sweet, and now you know why I insisted on no carnations in my wedding bouquet. The very sight of them brings the whole thing back, and all because I kept it to myself and *dwelled*. So you see I do know how you feel, but unless you put it out of your mind, or at least talk about it, it's going to leave a nasty blot on your subconscious. Don't you see?'

Dorothy nodded, clenching her hands until the nails bit into the palms.

'I see,' she said, 'and I'll try. Honestly I'll try.'

Margaret smiled on her with sisterly affection. 'And you don't need to worry about Mother finding out that Stanley came round tonight when she was out. I won't dream of telling, and Gerald won't mention it. He's more understanding than you think, you know. When we discussed it after you'd rushed out like that, do you know what he said?'

'What did he say?'

'"Forget it," he said. "They're only kids. As far as I'm concerned," he said, "there was no one in when we came back."' Margaret's voice held more than a touch of pride. 'Just think. He even smoked three cigarettes, one after the other, so that if Mother came back and smelt smoke, she wouldn't get suspicious. That's how considerate he is.'

She came over to where Dorothy sat dejectedly on the edge of the bed and touched her sister's hair in a fleeting caress. 'So stop looking so solemn, love. Just think of the nice things that are happening to us all, and about all the nice things to come. At the end of the summer I'll be married and living in my own home; you'll have left school, and although you won't believe it now, you'll go out with simply lots of boys before you decide on the right one.' She walked over to the door and turned. 'And somewhere there's someone just as super as Gerald waiting for you, you'll see.'

163

Dorothy nodded. If Margaret didn't go away and leave her alone she felt that her head would drop clean off with the nodding of it. She stretched her mouth into what she hoped would pass for a smile. 'All right, I'll remember, Margaret. Good night.'

Then listening intently until she heard the bathroom door open and close, Dorothy unlocked the wardrobe and took the cuff-link out of her blazer pocket. Stared down at it with distaste and subdued a sudden urge to open the window and hurl it away, out of sight. What had she done? Oh, dear God, what had she done? Then, thinking she heard a noise, she quickly replaced it, and locking the wardrobe again took the key out and put it underneath her pillow. A quick and necessary dash to the toilet whilst Margaret was closeted in the bathroom, and then a swift undressing and a dive into bed, without washing or cleaning her teeth.

When her mother called out to her from the landing half an hour later, she pulled the sheet over her head and pretended to be asleep. But she knew that if it had been her father's voice the temptation to talk to him would have overwhelmed her. Seeing his kindly face bending over her with concern she would have surely blurted out the whole mixed-up and unbelievable story from start to finish. Because then he would have sorted it out for her, the way he had always sorted things out for her since she was a child.

And when at long last she slept, it was to dream of Gerald, down on his knees in the middle of a field, praying to his own particular God, with his hands clasped in supplication, the red hairs sprouting sickeningly from between his knuckles. . . .

It was Church Parade the next morning, and when they arrived at the weathered stone church, the Guides and Brownies were already in their allotted pews at the front, with Philip's Vera in her Guide Captain's uniform at the end of a row, the navy-blue felt hat with its brim turned up at one side, squashed down over the whirls of plaits covering her ears.

Under her stern vigilance, the Guides sat straight and unsmiling in three solemn rows, but in front of them the Brownies held little whispered and giggling conversations together, their brown knitted caps bobbing animatedly.

Margaret, wearing a powder-blue coat with a matching hat shaped like a shallow dish with a feather going straight up at the side, glanced over at the Brownies and smiled at Dorothy. The smile said, 'Aren't they sweet?' and was calculated to show that no grim memories were troubling her that lovely spring morning. She lowered her head over her hands for a brief moment, then turned and smiled at the pew behind. Even the large urn of well-spaced-out carnations and greenery by the altar steps did nothing to dim the brightness of her smile, Dorothy noted.

Margaret was happy and wanted everyone to share in her happiness. Gerald would be waiting outside the church for her in his red car after the service, and in six weeks' time she would stand by his side and become his wife. Till death did them part.

Dorothy, reading her sister's mind with accuracy, bowed her head in prayer.

'Oh, God,' she prayed. 'Let me pass the cuff-link over to Beryl without anyone noticing. Give me a chance to persuade her how important it is that she puts it back. And please, God, forgive me for meddling. Forgive me for letting this awful imagination of mine run away with me, and let them find the man who killed Ruby quickly, so that Margaret's Gerald will be shown to be innocent, and forgive me for thinking that he had anything to do with it. Let it be that I turned him into a murderer in my mind because I don't want him to marry my sister. Like something out of Margaret's library book, as she explained. And tell Grandpa Bolton, if he's up there with you, to stop nudging me and putting thoughts in my head, and words in my mouth. For the sake of your son, Jesus Christ, amen.'

And watching her younger daughter's apparent devotion,

Phyllis smiled to herself, well satisfied.

The child was merely going through a phase, that was all. Adolescence was a difficult time, she mused, twiddling with a pearl ear-ring that was in danger of coming adrift. Like the menopause, adolescence affected some worse than others. She stole a sideways glance at her elder daughter. Margaret, bless her, now she had never been adolescent. Not a moment's worry since she was born. Phyllis looked up at the stained-glass window above the altar, depicting the Good Shepherd with the lost lamb in his arms. The colours were beautiful, especially with the sun slanting through them like that. Yes, it would be a worthy setting for the wedding ceremony. Margaret's train would look lovely as it fanned out behind her as she walked with Gerald to be prayed over after they'd been pronounced man and wife. That would be the moment when the choir in their red surplices sang *Love Divine* in charming descant. And how beautifully the red roses in Margaret's bouquet would tone in with the surplices, and how wise Gerald was to have decided on pale grey for his morning suit. With his red hair it would be just perfect. Phyllis sighed with contentment, then narrowed her eyes as her sister Ethel walked past the end of the pew accompanied by her husband. . . .

What was Ethel thinking about, wearing a purple hat to a dusty-pink coat? Really, she had no idea of what went with what, no idea of style at all. Goodness knows what she'd look like at the wedding, and goodness knows, Phyllis thought with pleasant smugness, what Beryl would look like in her bridesmaid's dress, even though she had given strict instructions to the dressmaker to go easy on the gathers round the second bridesmaid's dress.

She started as she felt Dorothy plucking at her sleeve.

'Where's Beryl?' she was whispering. 'Why isn't she with Auntie Ethel and Uncle Raymond? I saw her yesterday and she said she'd be at church this morning. Why isn't she . . . ?'

The row of worshippers in the pew in front stood up, and as the processional came slowly from the vestry, the rest of the congregation scrambled to their feet, searching for the right place in their prayer books.

And with anguish eating into her heart, and a mist of fear clouding her eyes, Dorothy stared down at the familiar words, her imagination taking wings again, soaring to the high dome of the ancient church.

'Oh, God,' she prayed as the congregation sank to their knees, 'don't let Gerald find that the cuff-link is missing. Let him decide to wear one of his sports shirts with buttons on the cuffs today. And, dear Lord, if he should discover that it's gone, make him think that he's forgotten where he put it. And let him be innocent of any involvement with Stanley's poor dead sister. Let him be hateful and slimy, and a liar with a sordid past, but don't let him have been Ruby Armstrong's lover. And let this be a lesson to me for allowing this terrible imagination of mine to run away with me. And if Grandpa Bolton's up there with you, tell him to stop prompting me about Gerald. Tell him that our Margaret loves him, and that he'll make her a good husband. Amen . . .'

The child is getting religious, Phyllis told herself, noticing the way Dorothy sank to her knees for the prayers, holding her hands piously over her face, and the way her lips moved during the reading from the Old Testament. She saw the way her younger daughter's eyes fixed themselves on the gold crucifix above the high altar, and the way her eyes filled with tears during the intoning of the Creed.

She wouldn't, she told herself bitterly, put it past Dorothy to do something absolutely beyond the pale, like wanting to turn Catholic. It would be just like her. And during the sermon she debated with herself which would be the worst, having a daughter who owed allegiance to the Pope, or one who boasted a mother-in-law who took in washing. She rose to her feet without having heard a single word of the vicar's short sermon, and sighed deeply. One thing she knew for sure, and that was that Dorothy would bring trouble. She felt in her bones that some way, somehow, this wilful child of hers would bring disgrace to them all.

'But let Margaret get married first,' was her final prayer. As the service ended, she collected gloves and handbag, and walked straight-backed from the church.

Fifteen

'The minute,' Phyllis said, 'the very minute we get into the house, Matthew, you must have a good talk to Dorothy. No wonder she's walking on in front of us like that. Just look at her slouching along and scuffing her best shoes. You'd think she was seven and not seventeen.'

They crossed the road from the church, and automatically Matthew did a little skip behind his wife to place himself on the kerb side of the pavement. Manners, he knew, mattered to Phyllis even when she was in the highest of dudgeons. And something had upset her good and proper this time. Her face was set into seething lines of anger, her mouth a thin grim line, and yet when the curate's wife rushed past en route for her kitchen and the Sunday dinner, Phyllis gave her a dazzling smile and even agreed that it was indeed a lovely day.

By heck, but she knew how to play to the gallery, Matthew thought wryly. There were times when he'd back his missus against Greta Garbo any old day.

'First she argues with our Ethel. Telling her she wants to see their Beryl, when all the time Ethel was explaining that Beryl would have gone over to Laurel Road to Raymond's sister's for their dinner. "She promised me she'd be at church this morning," she kept saying, as if Beryl could help waking up with one of her funny turns.'

'But if Beryl's well enough to go out for her dinner, surely she was well enough to go to church,' Matthew said mildly, feeling in his bones that he was missing the point, as usual.

169

'You're missing the point, as usual. Where Beryl had gone didn't come into it. The thing was that Dorothy should have accepted it, not gone on and on. I never thought she was all that close to Beryl, anyway.'

A woman in a yellow dress, holding a child by the hand, came out of a gate as they walked past, and Phyllis gave her a dazzling smile. 'She'll be our next president of the Inner Wheel,' she said in her normal voice, then resumed in a careful whisper. 'And then when our Margaret tried to persuade her to get into Gerald's car to go with them to the house, she actually knocked her hand away. Don't tell me you didn't see that.'

'I was talking to Raymond. Things are bad down at the yard. He says there's no orders coming in at all.'

'I don't blame Gerald entirely for saying what he did, though I must say I was surprised. The worst thing was that our Ethel heard him, and that was bad enough. Her eyebrows almost disappeared underneath that atrocious hat.'

'What *did* he say?' Matthew felt obliged to ask. 'Raymond says he had to lay off four more men last week.'

Phyllis sniffed. 'Raymond exaggerates, always has. Gerald, for your information, looked at Dorothy and said, "Either get in the bloody car, or stay out; either way makes no difference to me."'

'And what did our Dorothy say to that?'

'She told him to go to hell.'

'Are you sure it's not you who's exaggerating now, love?'

'I only wish I was.' Phyllis increased her pace to keep up with her rising anger. 'I've never been so humiliated in my whole life. And outside church too. Fancy coming straight out of church and using language like that.'

'Well, Gerald hadn't been to church,' Matthew said mildly, 'though I admit there's no love lost between him and Dorothy. Still, he's a lot older than she is, and he shouldn't have spoken to her like that.'

'She *provoked* him. She's always provoking him. She's one

170

on her own is our Dorothy. I can't think who she takes after . . . If she didn't look so much like Margaret I'd wonder sometimes if they gave me the wrong baby in the Nursing Home. I can't think of anybody on either side who she takes after. Did you see her in church? Down on her knees praying as if she was half way to a nunnery, then behaving like someone not in their right mind outside.'

They turned the corner into their own tree-lined road, and Matthew did his little sideways skip again as they crossed to the other side.

'And I wish you'd stop twiddling about like that,' Phyllis said ungratefully. 'It gets on my nerves. First I'm talking to you, then you're gone. No, it's the company our Dorothy's been keeping . . . and before you remind me about that boy out of Inkerman Street having won a scholarship to Oxford, let me remind you that breeding can't be learnt from books. It's inborn. And if she thinks I'm going to have him up to the house, she's another think coming. And if all she wants to do with her life is to mix with the working class, snogging on the back row of the pictures on a Saturday night, and standing in shop doorways, doing goodness knows what – oh yes, I wasn't born yesterday, Matthew – well, all I can say is that we've failed. We've given her everything, and all she wants to do is to throw it all back in our faces.'

Matthew sighed. 'Surely things aren't as bad as that, love? I admit she's been behaving a bit strangely these past few days, but what can you expect? Ruby Armstrong's murder came too near for comfort. Can't you see? Dorothy, in spite of all your wishful thinking, was *involved*. She was actually talking to the brother a few yards away from where they found the body, tha knows.' His wife's eyebrows rose at the slip into dialect, but he took no notice. More was at stake, he felt, than him minding his ps and qs. 'It wasn't just a sordid crime she read about in the paper; it happened to the sister of someone she knew very well. She's about the same age as that poor lass, give or take a year or two, and it isn't easy to take a thing like that in your stride, love. Not at seventeen.'

He clicked open the gate, and held it wide for his wife to pass through, raising his trilby hat to the man next door who was cutting his hedge. Then, lowering his voice, he said, 'I haven't managed to fathom it out yet, but I feel that our Dorothy's contrasting the fuss about the wedding with that poor lass's fate. Perhaps for the first time in her life she's finding out that life isn't fair, that it never was and never will be.' He stood back to let Phyllis go before him into the house. 'Leave her be, love, and it'll all blow over, you'll see.'

'She's gone straight upstairs,' Phyllis said, after a quick peep into the downstairs rooms. 'If I hadn't to see to the joint I'd have a word with her myself, but what I have to say will keep.' She took off her hat and patted her hair back into shape. 'You go up and see if you can talk some sense into her.' She handed her coat over to him. 'And make sure you hang this on a padded hanger, please.' Her eyes met his in honest bewilderment. 'And why that poor girl getting herself murdered should have anything whatsoever to do with our Margaret getting married, beats me. Margaret didn't even know her.' She walked with her quick light step towards the kitchen. 'And if Dorothy doesn't behave herself at the table I'll send her upstairs, whether she's seventeen or not.'

Hauling himself up by the bannister as if it were a ropeladder on a ship and not a wide polished piece of oak, Matthew went heavily upstairs. Trying to talk sense into Phyllis when she was in this mood was nigh impossible. He'd be glad when this wedding was over, by heck he would. He'd offered Margaret all the money the reception at The Pied Bull was going to cost, plus another two hundred for the fancy clothes and what not, and suggested that she eloped with Gerald.

'Don't be funny, Father,' she'd said, but he hadn't been trying to be funny. At the moment he'd meant it, from the bottom of his heart. He paused at the bend of the stairs, feeling the familiar tightness in his chest, as if there were an elastic band squeezing the breath out of him. By heck but he were out of condition, right enough. He unbuttoned his waistcoat. In a way he could side with Dorothy, if that was the reason for her behaving so strangely these past few days. It did seem all wrong to be spending money as if it were water on a fancy wedding, when the dole queues were stretching half way round the Labour Exchange and right down Queen Street. Men with brown paper tacked inside their vests, and pieces of cardboard shoved inside their shoes to keep out the cold, working on their allotments and their hen-pens all day long to try and eke out their meagre intake of food with vegetables, and a chicken at Christmas if they were lucky. And the way things were going, it looked as if Raymond might have to close down in the not too distant future. He sighed as he continued his way upstairs. He'd be all right, Raymond would; he'd more than a bob or two put by, but some of his men had been with the firm since leaving school, and had felt secure enough to start buying their own houses. By the heck, it didn't bear thinking about. . . .

Wearily he went into the bedroom and sitting down on the edge of the double bed, crossed one leg awkwardly over the other and began to pick at the knot in his shoe-laces. He supposed he'd better have a word with Dorothy, partly to pacify Phyllis, and partly because he was a bit worried about her himself. He hadn't wanted to add fuel to the fire by admitting that he had seen a bit of what had gone on outside the church out of the corner of his eye when he'd been talking to Raymond. But it were right enough that there were no love lost between his younger daughter and Margaret's intended. For one startled moment he'd thought they were going to come to blows, matching up to one another on the pavement, for all the world like two fighting cocks. He eased his feet into his slippers. There was a lot of his father in Dorothy, and that was a fact. If the old man had taken it into his head to dislike someone, then that

173

was it. No compromise; no being pleasant just for the sake of appearances.

'He don't like me, and I don't like him,' he remembered his father saying once about a completely inoffensive little tackler at the mill. 'And that's bloody that.'

'But there's such a thing as tolerance, and live and let live,' Matthew muttered to himself as he went out on to the landing and knocked on the door of Dorothy's room. And the sooner this lass of his grew up a bit and realized it, the better for all of them. . . .

And, so preoccupied that he forgot to wait for Dorothy's voice telling him to come in, Matthew opened the door and walked straight into the bedroom.

Dorothy was lying flat on her bed still wearing her shoes and her blazer, her toes pointing up to the ceiling, and her face drained of colour. She didn't turn her head, and Matthew doubted if she'd even heard him come in. Just for a moment the elastic band tightened itself round his heart again as he looked at her. By the heck, but there was summat wrong all right. Summat serious too. This was more than one of her Bolshie moods. More than an idealistic aversion to wedding preparations taking precedence over Ruby Armstrong's murder. His lass was in real trouble, and if that lad from down Inkerman Street had been up to owt with her, he'd tear him limb from limb, and he wouldn't even wait till 'funeral were over tomorrow either. Matthew walked towards the bed. But she weren't like that, not his Dorothy. She were nobbut a child, and as pure as the driven snow; he'd stake his life on that.

Sitting down on the bed, which creaked in protest, he patted her hand. 'Now then, chuck, let's have it. However bad it is, let's have it straight. There's nowt so terrible that can't be put right. Not now your old dad's here. Come on now, tell me all about it.'

Dorothy's other hand, the one in her pocket, curled round the cuff-link. Slowly, as if she was dreaming, she turned her head and stared at her father. And the terrible anxiety on his red face broke down her defences, so that she sat up and threw herself against him, burying her head in the tobacco-smelling comfort of his old cardigan, at the same time as his arms came round her and held her tight.

'I can't tell you,' she sobbed when the first bout of crying was over. 'It's so awful. I can't begin.'

Matthew rocked her gently, backwards and forwards, knowing from experience that she would have to get her cry over and done with first. It had always been the same, ever since she was a little lass. First the explosive torrent of tears, the passionate unburdening of whatever was troubling her, then the whispered expression of her feelings. And half an hour afterwards, he reminded himself, the swift return to normality, with her pinched smile at variance with the swollen eyelids and little tear-blotched face.

Dear God, he asked himself silently, why did this one of his chicks have to be so vulnerable? Why did she have to get herself so *involved*? By heck, but life was going to hurt her badly. If it hadn't hurt her already . . . He held her away from him, trying to get her to look at him, but her head dropped down to her chest.

'Is it anything to do with that lad? That Stanley?' he said, dreading what she might be going to tell him, but knowing that there'd be no peace for either of them till it was said.

'In a way.' She gulped. 'In a way it has.'

Matthew patted her head. 'Take your time, love, come on now, get it over with, and whatever it is we'll have it put right. There's nowt so bad as can't be mended, you know that.'

'It's . . . it's about Gerald. Gerald Tomlin . . .'

'Aye?' Matthew's voice soothed and encouraged, showing nothing of the surprise he felt, and into his shoulder Dorothy made her confession.

'I think I've always known that he was meeting girls from the mill – oh, before he got engaged to our Margaret. He used to take them for drives in his car; he almost admitted it to me himself, but that wouldn't have mattered, because he

175

loves our Margaret, I'm sure of that, but I think that one of the weavers he was meeting was Ruby Armstrong.'

'Go on.' Matthew's voice held a grim note now.

'I think he was meeting her secretly, right up to getting engaged three months ago, then, give him his due, he stopped seeing her, but then I think . . . I've worked it out that when Ruby found out for sure that she was pregnant, she persuaded him to see her. Just once.'

Matthew stopped the rocking motion, and held her very still.

'I even think it may have been the night she died, because Beryl told me he lied to the police. Not a big lie, just saying he went for a drive when really he went for a walk. She watches him go out, you know, from the landing window.'

'Carry on.'

'Stanley told me that a weaver from the mill was standing at the West Road gate of the park that night with a boy, and she thought she saw someone like Ruby going into the park, with a boy. Or a man.'

'And does Stanley know all this, then?'

'Not about Gerald lying to the police. I only found that out after he'd . . . afterwards.' She paused for a moment. 'And he, Gerald, he lost a cuff-link, one of the pair Margaret bought him for their engagement present.' Her hand crept into her pocket again. 'And he went down to Mr Adamson's shop and replaced it. But he's still searching for it, because I've figured out that he can't think where he lost it. So he's still searching in his room.'

'And how do you know that, love?'

'Beryl. She watches him.'

'Why?'

'Because she has a crush on him. She's like that. And yesterday she saw him in the park, after she'd been playing tennis, and she said he was walking along a path with his head bent. Near the duck pond.'

'Bit of a long shot, chuck?'

'Not when you're desperate.'

176

'And Beryl knows what you think?'

Dorothy shook her head. 'I'm not that daft, am I?'

Matthew took a deep breath. 'It's dangerous thinking, lovey. You know that, don't you?'

Dorothy nodded into his shoulder. 'I know, and I haven't finished yet.' She let out a shuddering sigh. 'Last night I went round to Beryl's house when Auntie Ethel and Uncle Raymond were out, and I stole the odd cuff-link from his room.'

'You what?'

'I did. I didn't mean to take it, but I thought I heard someone coming and I panicked and put it in my pocket, and I meant to give it back to Beryl this morning after church and get her to put it back, but she wasn't there, and then when I saw Gerald he looked at me as if he hated my guts and swore at me, and I think he may have found out what I did.' She moved against him. 'I think Beryl might have told him, even though I got her to swear on the Bible that she wouldn't.'

Matthew closed his eyes.

'And now you're not sure? Is that what you're trying to tell me, then?'

She nodded. 'I prayed and prayed in church that I'm wrong, and if I am, and if he's found out that I was in his room last night, I still have to explain how I came to take the cuff-link, and I can't. And I'm so mixed up I don't know what I am, or whether what I think is real or just in my imagination any more. And don't tell Mother, but Stanley came round last night when you were out, and he says that even accusing Gerald in my mind is dangerous. But Gerald Tomlin knew Stanley's sister all right. Even if he didn't meet her that night, he knew her. And he could be the father of Ruby's baby. I know it inside me. It all fits.'

Then at last she lifted her head, and over her father's shoulder saw her mother standing in the doorway.

Phyllis was wearing the frilly apron, tied in a neat bow at the back, looking so ordinary, so much her meticulously organized self that, when she spoke, the voice that came as a low growl from her throat startled Matthew so much that he stood up, unable to utter a word himself, moving his big head from side to side in a desperate fashion.

How long had she been there? Had she heard what had been said? And if she had, then heaven help them.

He moved towards her, holding out his hand, but she ignored him as if he wasn't in the room at all.

Dorothy slid from the bed and faced her mother, her head up, not as much in defiance as in fear. Her mother's face was contorted almost out of recognition with a rage so terrible it seemed to leap from her throat like a living thing.

'You wicked, wicked little devil! You brazen, interfering little sod! How dare you suggest that Gerald had anything to do with that young whore from down Inkerman Street?' She put up a hand as if to ward off anything Dorothy or her father might say. 'Who, I ask you, but the devil himself could have put such thoughts into your head? You . . . you little bugger.'

'Don't swear, Mother.'

It was a foolish thing to say, but Dorothy never remembered her prunes and prism mother uttering so much as a 'damn'. It was as though Phyllis was possessed. And if the devil was in that room at that moment, he was in her mother's heart, not her own. She swayed where she stood. 'But, listen, Mother. I don't know for sure . . . I said I didn't know. But I had to find out. For Margaret's sake, I had to . . .'

'Shut up!' Phyllis took a menacing step forwards. 'How dare you even mention your sister's name after what you've just said? Don't you know, or have you forgotten, that her wedding-dress is hanging there in the spare room? And even at this very minute she's with that decent young man looking over the house they're going to live in together?' She narrowed her eyes. 'I knew this morning, even as you knelt by my side in church, that you were up to something. Muttering your mealy-mouthed prayers, you little sod.

178

And I'll tell you what's wrong with you, what's always been wrong with you. You're jealous of your sister. Jealous as hell. Jealous because she's going to marry a fine man, and jealous because as far as disposition goes you're not fit to grovel at her feet and lick her big toe. You've been against this wedding right from the start, and now you think you've found a way to bugger it all up.' Her voice rose. 'Aye, and bugger us all up too. Not content with mixing with the scum of the earth yourself, you want the rest of your family to be dragged down with you. And I suppose you've told Beryl all this cock-and-bull story? That's what you were saying, wasn't it?'

'I haven't. I only said I thought that Gerald . . .'

'I said shut up!' Phyllis's face was as frightening as her voice now, all pretence at refinement gone. 'Aye, you'd like that,' she went on. 'You'd like your Auntie Ethel to think we were mixed up in a bit of muckiness, wouldn't you? You'd like them to think we've been taken down a peg, wouldn't you?'

'Oh, Mother, please . . .'

'Don't you try to come the little innocent with me now, Dorothy Bolton. Only somebody with a sick mind could have dreamed up the story I heard you tell your father just now. Inferring that Gerald had something to do with that sordid murder . . . and when they come back from the house I want you gone. Go where you bloody well like, but I'm not having you sitting at my dinner table with thoughts like that in your head.'

Matthew put out his hand to touch her, but she knocked it away with a fierce slicing motion.

He tried again. 'Come now, lass. It were a shock hearing it like that. It's been a shock to me, and I'm sure that Gerald's done nothing very terrible. But it needs sorting out . . .'

'Not this time, Matthew. This time you can't sort anything out. Because the only one that needs sorting out is her.'

And as Dorothy took a step forward Phyllis's fist shot out and caught her full on the mouth, and as she cried aloud and tried to shield herself with her arms, Phyllis took hold of her by the shoulders and shook her so that her teeth rattled and the blood spun in her head.

It was like a drunken street brawl, a Saturday night punch-up down in the main streets of the town, with Matthew, galvanized into action at last, pinning his wife's arms behind her back. With Dorothy rushing headlong from the room, stumbling down the stairs, wrenching at the big front door, and running out into the bright spring sunshine, with no thought in her head but that she must get away. . . .

Sixteen

For what seemed like an eternity, but could in reality have been only a few seconds, Matthew felt as if he was being split into two people. One half of him was running down the stairs after Dorothy, and the other half was ministering to his wife, trying to calm her into some sort of normality.

And staying where he was in the bedroom he could still see himself, in his mind's eye, calling Dorothy's name, with the neighbours looking up from their hedge-trimming, and coming from their Sunday dinners, to see who was making all that commotion in the normally quiet, respectable road.

'I'd never have caught up with her,' he muttered to himself as he tried to draw Phyllis into the circle of his arms, straining at her as she stiffened against him.

'I blame you for this,' she said, quieter now, but still speaking in that rough, alien voice. 'You've spoilt her since the day she was born. Giving in to her whims and making excuses for her.' She started to whimper. 'We were too old; we're too old to cope, there's too much of your father in her. There's bad blood somewhere there.'

'Rubbish.' Matthew wished he could sit down, but it didn't seem the right time, even though his legs felt as if they were weighted with lead. 'You'd no right to hit her,' he said sadly. 'She's not a child. You'd no right to land out at her like that.'

Phyllis turned her back on him and walked her straight-backed walk to the door. To his amazement he could see that already her normal self-control was asserting itself,

181

and the immediate transition from a shouting virago to her customary prim refinement seemed so shocking that he felt a physical churning of disgust in his stomach.

Groping for the bannister he followed her down the stairs, fumbling with his feet for each step like a blind man as she talked at him over her shoulder.

'Margaret and Gerald will be back at any minute, and they mustn't suspect that anything's been happening. Not by any sign at all must they suspect that we've had words.' She turned at the bottom of the stairs, and her face was as smooth as if they'd had a slight difference of opinion about whether to open a tin of peaches or a tin of pineapple for pudding. 'We'll tell them that Dorothy had a telephone call from a friend, and has gone there for dinner.'

'Just like that?' Matthew followed her into the kitchen.

'Yes, just like that,' Phyllis said, taking the oven gloves down from the hook by the gas-oven and thrusting her hands inside them. Then before bending down to open the oven door she stared straight at him with a direct look that started the churning sensation in his middle once again.

'What our Dorothy said was never said. It's gone. Done with, and never to be referred to again. Not ever. And when she comes back you can tell her that yourself because it will be a long time before I can trust myself to speak to her . . .'

Matthew took his handkerchief from his trouser pocket and wiped his forehead, and if anything at all had been registering in his wife's mind at that moment she would have seen the way he sank down on to a kitchen chair, and seen the greyness of his usually ruddy cheeks, and the way his mouth had fallen slack and strangely blue.

'And Dorothy?' he asked. 'Don't you even care where she's gone?'

Phyllis took a ladle and started to baste the sizzling joint of beef, spooning the hot fat over it with a hand as steady as a rock.

'You know as well as I do where she'll have gone to. Down Inkerman Street. To that boy. To where she belongs.

And as far as I'm concerned she can stay there.'

Matthew blinked hard as if to get her into focus. This was his wife, the mother of his two daughters. The mother of Dorothy as well as of Margaret. He blinked his eyes again.

'And if she repeats what she said?'

'She said nothing!'

Matthew spoke slowly but clearly as if trying to make himself understood to a backward five-year-old child. 'Dorothy is headstrong, and foolish at times, we both know that, but however terrible the consequences might be, lass, we've got to talk about what she said. We've got to talk it out between the three of us even if it's just the means of setting it right between her and Gerald. She'll be coming back.' He turned his head as if already he heard his daughter's returning footsteps. 'She always comes back, after all she's run down the road in a flaming temper more times than Gerald's had hot dinners. I know, I know. This time she's gone too far, this time that imagination of hers has really gone off the rails, and she's been foolish and impulsive, but it's got to be thrashed out. If Gerald . . .' He licked his dry lips. 'If Gerald had been seeing that poor lass – and what he did before he started courting our Margaret seriously is his own concern; he's not a mere slip of a lad you know, and I wasn't born yesterday either, I've seen the way he stares at a pretty girl.' Matthew recoiled from his wife's glare. 'Nay, lass, there's no need to look like that. The man what doesn't look twice at a pretty lass might as well go into a corner and roll up then stiffen himself. But if Gerald *did* meet the Armstrong lass, well, he's got to be a man and own up. He's got to tell the police because – don't you see, chuck? – it could give them a lead as to who she was seeing – who she saw that night.'

'Gerald is not the type of young man to associate with your weavers,' Phyllis stressed each word. 'And Dorothy said *nothing*. And if she opens her mouth outside this house then my door will never open to her again. Never.'

Matthew sighed. He'd read somewhere once that under

great stress people could blank out a part of their minds, refusing to believe, or unable to believe that which they refused to acknowledge to be truth. But this was Phyllis. His wife. A woman with predictable reactions to any given situation. Narrow-minded and bigoted maybe, but predictable.

'You don't mean that, love,' he said, shaking his big head from side to side. Then, as the sound of the front door opening and closing cut short another spate of angry words, he saw the way Phyllis arranged her face into a smile of welcome, a smile which made him recoil and put up a hand to his mouth as if she had hit out at him also.

Margaret came straight through the hall into the kitchen, swinging her Sunday hat in her hand, her coat unbuttoned, glowing with the special kind of happiness that Gerald seemed to be able to instil in her. Her voice held a teasing quality. 'Here you both are, then, looking as guilty as a pair of old Nicks. What's been going on?'

'Going on, dear?' Phyllis's smile cracked a little at the corners. 'What do you mean? There's nothing been going on, has there, Father?'

Margaret sniffed the air with appreciation. 'Gosh, but that smells good. We were driving up Steep Brow just now when we saw our Dorothy walking down the other side, and though I swear she saw us, she turned her head away and started to run.' She turned to Phyllis. 'You've found out, I suppose?'

'Found out what?' Phyllis's smile disappeared as if someone had stepped forward and wiped it from her face with a damp flannel.

'About that Stanley boy coming round to the house last night when you were out. Good heavens, there's no need to look like that, the pair of you. Dorothy isn't the first girl to have a boy in when she's alone, and she won't be the last. He looks harmless enough, honestly.' She laughed and ran her fingers through her hair. 'Can't you see that if you ignore him he'll disappear? He isn't Dorothy's type, I can tell you that. Gerald and I are always saying that she'll have to find a boy who can dominate her before she can respect him, and this boy definitely isn't the domineering type. It was funny really, the way they scuttled out when we came in. Like two frightened rabbits.'

Matthew found his voice at last. 'Where's Gerald then? Making sure the car's all right? I didn't hear you drive in.'

Margaret turned to go upstairs. 'Gone after Dorothy, of course. He'll calm her down if anyone can. He dropped me off at the end of the road, then he reversed round the corner and went after her. Want to bet that by the time I've set the table she's back, pleading to be forgiven?' She put her head on one side and glanced at them mischievously from beneath her eyelashes. 'You are a fuddy-duddy pair. Can't you see that she's a bit upset with that awful thing happening in the park? There's nothing for you to look so worried about. Honestly.'

And as the soft click of her bedroom door closed behind her the door-bell rang. Apologetically, as if someone had merely brushed the bell with a finger, then regretted it immediately.

'He's found her already.' Matthew closed both eyes with the enormity of his relief.'

'I tell you, Matthew. If she says as much as a word . . .'

'You get on with the dinner.' He walked heavily out of the kitchen and down the hall, his step faltering as he opened the door and saw the bulky form of his friend Arnold Bates, standing there on the step, as obviously a policeman as if he was wearing full uniform and not the tweed suit with the canary-yellow waistcoat and the watch-chain draped across his ample middle. Profusely apologetic, he stood there in the Sunday sunshine, twisting the brim of a brown trilby hat round and round in his hands.

'Morning, Matthew.'

Almost without volition, Matthew pulled the big door partially closed behind him. 'Morning, Arnold.'

'Looks like summer's come at last.'

'Aye. Not before time though.'

'But there's still a nip in the air if tha' moves out of the sun.'

'Aye, that's right.'

'Missus well?'

'Aye. And Gertie?'

'Fair to middlin'. Still has her usual rheumatism about this time of the year. Always at its worst when 'weather perks up.'

Then Sergeant Bates looked his old friend in the eye. 'I've come on a tricky errand, Matthew. Just come from your brother-in-law's house. Tha knows. Raymond Rostron,' he added unnecessarily.

Matthew found he was holding his breath. 'They've gone out for their dinner, but they'll be back about three no doubt. Hope there's nowt wrong down at the yard. Raymond's worried enough without any trouble in that direction.'

The sergeant shook his head. 'Aye, well.' Then he studied a loose piece of gravel on the path with intense concentration. 'Well, it were really their lodger I wanted to see. Mr Gerald Tomlin.' He kicked the gravel furiously with the toe of a well-polished shoe. 'Your lass's intended. Tha' knows?'

Matthew glanced over his shoulder. There was no need for him to be holding his breath now. It was holding itself, or so it seemed. 'He's not here,' he whispered. His voice sounded as if it was coming from a long way. 'But he'll be here soon. Aye, that's right. He'll be coming soon. He's coming here for his dinner.'

'Good.' Sergeant Bates avoided his eyes, staring now with interest at the tip of a thumb-nail. 'Then I'll come inside and wait if tha' doesn't mind. There's just one or two questions I'd like to ask him. Routine tha' knows, purely routine.'

'In connection with Ruby Armstrong's murder?'

The words were out before Matthew could stop them,

before he even knew his mind had formed them, and completely oblivious to the sudden narrowing of the sergeant's eyes, he stepped round him and strode quickly to the gate. Straining his eyes against the sun, he stared down the road, anticipating the roar of the engine in Gerald's red car, praying that it might turn the corner, *willing* it to appear.

And seeing and hearing nothing . . .

Seventeen

Although Dorothy was walking in the direction of Inkerman Street, she was doing so without intent. Walking
aimlessly as the despairing do, putting one foot in front of
the other, her mind at times a blank and at times seething
with resentment.

In the last hour, since coming out of church, the wind
had dropped, and the midday sun, high in the sky, was
warm on her shoulders.

'Don't like it when it comes too soon,' a woman was
telling her next-door neighbour as she stood, arms folded,
squinting at the clear blue sky.

'Aye, we're bound to suffer for it later,' her neighbour
said, going inside and closing the door on the sunshine.

Dorothy, hands deep in her blazer pocket, turned into
Balaclava Street, walking with head bent so that she almost
stumbled over a chair placed in front of a bay window. A
woman, shelling peas into a white basin, grinned at her. 'If
this is going to be summer, then I'm making sure I'm on
'front row for it.'

Dorothy smiled back at her automatically . . . Mother
would have been horrified. In Phyllis's code, to sit out at the
back of the house was in order if one was decently screened
from one's neighbours. But to sit out at the *front* of the house
put one entirely beyond the pale.

'Oh, Mother . . .' she muttered, walking straight into
the chalked-in squares of a hopscotch game, causing a tiny
girl, balancing on one foot in a numbered flagstone, to

shout out in indignant protest: 'Left yer glasses at home, then?'

'Sorry.' Dorothy walked on. 'Sorry . . . sorry.'

Sorry she'd made such a mess of things, sorry she'd upset her mother so much, sorry for herself, sorry for Stanley. Sorry for the whole terrible, terrible mess.

'But she shouldn't have hit me . . .' Her mouth hurt and she could feel the swelling where her top teeth had caught her lip at the unexpected violence of the blow. People didn't hit people. Not Phyllis's kind. A woman like Phyllis was always in control; even a flash of temper showing merely as a tightening of the lips, a narrowing of the eyes.

It wasn't dignified . . . she had known exactly where she stood with her mother, knew exactly how far she could go. Now she felt as if she had never really known her mother, and as if she would never really know her again.

And she'd have to go back. She had known she would have to go back, even before she'd reached the end of her road. The white-hot flame of her own anger was dying down, the grand dramatic gesture of flinging herself out of the house was being superseded by a feeling of embarrassment. Embarrassment and a slow acknowledgement of her own sound common sense.

If she didn't go back, then where *could* she go?

Certainly not to Stanley's house, even though her footsteps had instinctively led her in that direction. They had enough to worry them with the funeral tomorrow. Not to Cousin Beryl's house because they had gone out to dinner. To Mrs Wilkinson's?

'Please, Mrs Wilkinson, may I come in? My mother's hit me across the mouth and told me to bugger off.'

No, Phyllis ought not to have hit her. It wasn't right. They weren't supposed to do things like that in the red-brick houses up by the park. Without realizing it, Dorothy began to whimper.

'Anything wrong, chuck?' A man with a narrow grey face, with a flat cap pulled low down over his eyes, leaned back against a window-bottom, smoking a Woodbine tucked neatly into the curved palm of his hand.

Shaking her head, Dorothy walked on quickly.

Oh no, there was nothing wrong. She'd only put the cat amongst the pigeons, as Grandpa Bolton would have said. Oh no, nothing wrong. Just that she'd done it this time, done it right and proper. Her fingers curled over the cuff-link down in the patch pocket of her blazer as she walked over to the edge of the pavement, staring down at a grate.

All she had to do was to drop the cuff-link between the grids, watch it disappear, and the evidence, if evidence it was, would be gone for ever. She teetered on the kerb, swaying slowly backwards and forwards.

Then she lifted her head and saw Gerald's red car cruising leisurely down the street towards her.

'Tha'd best come in here, Arnold.'

Matthew led the way into the lounge, the cosy, chintzy room bright with sunshine, the brasses round the massive cream tiled fireplace a-twinkle with the three monkeys on the mantelpiece shining in three-fold splendour.

Sergeant Bates, trilby hat still clutched in his hand, sat down on the very edge of the chesterfield, and refused a drink.

'Not when I'm on duty, Matthew, thanks all the same.'

'But surely . . .? Matthew took up his normal stance in front of the fireplace, hands clenched deep inside the cardigan pockets. Pulling it out of shape, as Phyllis would have said.

The sergeant coughed. 'The missus?' he asked.

'In the kitchen.' Matthew nodded towards the Westminster chime clock. 'It's nearly dinner-time.'

'Aye. Well . . .' Sergeant Bates started to spin his hat round at a feverish rate. 'This is a helluva spot for us both to be in, Matthew. I'd have given anything, anything, but with you being a pal and everything . . .' He looked up and sighed. 'I've left the car outside Raymond's house.'

Matthew walked over to one of the easy chairs and perched himself awkwardly on the well-padded arm. He couldn't bring himself to sit down in it properly, not with part of him still straining after Dorothy. Not with part of him picturing Gerald searching the streets at the wheel of his red car. Gerald who . . . oh God!

'Say what tha's come to say, Arnold.' Then he forced himself to continue. 'Tha's taking him in. I'm right, aren't I?'

His solid homely face suffused with colour, the sergeant nodded. 'Aye, I'm afraid I am, lad.' He placed the trilby down on the cushion beside him, found he couldn't manage without it, and picked it up again, examining the brim with a look of intense concentration. 'I'm sorry, Matthew. Heart sorry I am. This is the hardest thing I've had to do ever since I were a bobby on the beat, but we've had our eye on him for a bit. Seems he had a bit of a field-day with some of the lasses at the mill when he first came up here.'

'But that doesn't make him a . . .' Matthew couldn't bring himself to say the word.

'No, it doesn't, but one or two of the things he told us didn't match up, then this morning, one of your weavers, a big blonde lass, came into the station with her father. Wouldn't talk to no one but me, so they sent for me. He'd made her come. Practically had to drag her through the streets, he said.'

'Mabel Earnshaw?'

'Aye. How did you know that, then?'

Matthew put one hand inside his cardigan, and rubbed his chest bone. 'She was a mate of Ruby Armstrong's, though I could never see what they saw in one another. One were as brash as t'other were reserved.'

'Aye. Well, it seems that Ruby had confided in the lass, this Mabel. Sworn her to secrecy 'bout three months back. Told her she was meeting Mr Tomlin on the sly. Said her mother would kill her if she found out.'

'She would 'n all.'

'Told her she was meeting him on the night.' The sergeant coughed and cleared his throat. 'On the night in question.'

Matthew got up from the arm of the chair and began to pace backwards and forwards. 'And she's kept quiet? It doesn't seem feasible. I can't believe that somehow. Can you?'

Sergeant Bates nodded. 'Seems Mr Tomlin saw her down at the mill the morning after, and managed to convince her that whilst he had indeed met Ruby, he had left her in the park. Swore it with tears in his eyes apparently, and convinced her that he had nothing to do with that poor lass's death.'

He twisted round to face Matthew, who was staring out of the window at the sun-drenched garden. 'Told her that if she said anything she would lose her job.'

'Oh, my God!' Matthew raised his voice. 'They know they only have to come to me.' Then he paused. 'She's not very bright, Mabel Earnshaw, but she's the only one working out of a big family. There have been times when I'd have sacked her, but knowing that . . .'

'Exactly. Seems her father's been out of work for three years, and the only money going into that house is what Mabel earns.'

'Bloody Means Test.' Matthew shook his head. 'But I still can't see how she could have kept quiet.' He lowered his head. 'She could have come to me. They allus know they can come to me.'

Sergeant Bates rubbed the finger and thumb of his right hand together, and Matthew interpreted the gesture at once.

'Blackmail? Oh, dear God in heaven!'

'Empty bellies have a special code of their own, Matthew. Seems one of the children has had consumption and needs proper food and milk. So there were no questions asked at home.'

'The mother. Don't know what she's like now, but she used to be a wrong 'un, Arnold. She'd ask no questions.'

The sergeant sniffed. 'Aye, they didn't call her tanner-a-time for nowt. But all the same I believe that lass when she said she doesn't believe that Mr Tomlin had anything to do with young Ruby Armstrong's death. "He's a proper gentleman," she kept saying over and over again.'

'But you think he did it?'

It seemed as though his world stood still, as though even the brasses round the fireplace stopped their twinkling as Matthew waited for the sergeant's reply.

'Arnold! How very nice.'

Phyllis's right hand was extended in a smiling welcome, her apron whisked off and held behind her back in deference to her unexpected visitor. Only an extra sharp brittleness in her speech giving away her agitation to her husband. She moved forward into the room. 'I thought I heard Matthew bringing someone in, but I was busy with the dinner. Just look at you sitting there without a drink in your hand, and this the cocktail hour.' She laughed nervously. 'Matthew, what can you be thinking about? And how's Gertrude? We're looking forward to seeing you at the wedding . . .'

'Sit down, love.'

Matthew spoke softly, but in a strange way his voice rang out like a pistol shot.

'I can't sit down now.' Phyllis flashed a brilliant smile at the sergeant. 'You men are all the same. You think a Sunday dinner appears on the table all by itself.' She walked towards the door, and something in the set of her shoulders told Matthew that she knew. Knew, and didn't wish to hear. Thought that, by walking away into the shining neatness of her kitchen, the terrible thing that was happening would be restored to pristine oblivion also. He felt behind him for the edge of a chair and sat down. Oh God, in Thy infinite mercy, have pity on her. What she had to hear would kill her, as stone-dead as if someone had fired a bullet straight at her heart.

193

He exchanged a glance and a quick nod with the sergeant.

'Phyllis. Come back here, love. There's something you have to know. Arnold isn't paying a social call, not this time.' He ran his tongue over his dry lips. 'It's about Gerald, love. Arnold's come about Gerald.'

'No!' Phyllis swung round. 'It's not true. She's made it all up, the little sod. She didn't waste much time running to you, did she? She must have well nigh burst her lungs running to the nearest telephone to spread that muck.' She stared wild-eyed at the astonished sergeant. 'And you believe her? You'd take notice of a little lying runt like that?'

Matthew reached for his wife, and although he could have sworn he was shouting, the words he spoke were no more than a whisper:

'It's got nothing to do with Dorothy, nothing. Listen, for God's sake. We've got to find her, because it looks like Gerald's gone after her. He suspects that she knows something, and he's gone after her.'

Sergeant Bates was at the door in two single strides. 'You tell me that now, Matthew! For God's sake, man, let's get going. Fast.'

With a tormented backwards glance at his wife, Matthew followed the burly figure of the sergeant out of the house, leaving Phyllis running upstairs, the adrenalin pumping so fast that it seemed her feet scarce touched the stairs. The one thought in her head was to get to Margaret, to hold her, to comfort her, to promise they'd go away, far away, and never come back. Never. Never.

And as she opened the bedroom door, she saw Margaret sitting serenely in front of her dressing-table, staring calmly at her reflection in the mirror, blue eyes smiling back in tranquil oblivion.

'Mother! I'm sorry. Is dinner ready? I was day-dreaming. Is Gerald back?'

Phyllis stumbled forward, holding out her arms. Then,

as her daughter turned round, she ran back along the wide landing, into the spare room where the white satin wedding-dress hung from the picture-rail, wrapped in its covering sheet. And pulling it down, she tore at the neckline with a strength that was more than human, felt the stitches give, and tore and tore, ripping, scrabbling at the fragile lace.

Then suddenly, as if pole-axed, she fell backwards on to the floor, eyes and mouth agape, the terrible turn of events for ever obliterated from her mind as she stared unseeing at the ceiling.

And it was Margaret who telephoned for the ambulance, dialling with trembling fingers, calling in vain for her father, sobbing for Gerald, for Dorothy – for anyone to come quickly. Seeing her whole world turned upside down, her happiness in jeopardy, as she knelt by her mother's still form and felt for a pulse that seemed to be non-existent.

'Get in!' Gerald Tomlin held the door of the red sports car open. 'Come on, you little ninny, I'll run you home.' He glanced at his wrist watch, pushing back a cuff to check the time, and Dorothy sighed with relief. Cuffs with buttons, she noticed thankfully.

He smiled at her. 'Five past one, and you know what your mother is about meals being on time. Come on. You don't want me to have to get out and lift you into the car, do you? We're getting some funny looks from across the street as it is, and it wouldn't look nice now on a Sunday, would it?'

Dorothy hesitated. She felt drained, as if someone had inserted a tap in her head and siphoned all her blood away. The anger had gone, evaporated away somehow into the clear blue sky, floating over the tall mill chimneys, and all that was left was a tired and sad bewilderment, and a numbness that the sun could do nothing to alleviate.

Gerald gave the door of the car an extra push. 'Well? Are you coming back of your own accord, or do I have to drag you by that golden hair of yours?' He grinned. 'Whatever's troubling you sweetie, don't let it spoil your dear mother's Sunday joint. It wouldn't be cricket now, would it?'

There was a woman standing at the door across the street eyeing them curiously, her arms folded across her flowered pinafore. Dorothy lifted her head. And the sun was shining, and Gerald Tomlin was the man her sister was going to marry and he might well have been a philanderer, but he couldn't have done that terrible thing. He was . . . he was a gentleman.

Sighing, as if somehow it had all been resolved without her having to do anything about it, Dorothy got into the car. It wouldn't be the first time she'd returned to the house with her tail between her legs. Flouncing out after a difference of opinion with her mother had come to be looked upon as a family joke. Once as a child, she remembered now, half smiling to herself, she had packed a case, squashing her teddy-bear in on top of her favourite book and her pyjamas and a frilly party dress. Then half way down the road she'd turned back again, taking her place at the table as if nothing had happened.

'That's better.' Gerald patted her knee, let in the clutch and drove away from the kerb. 'Sensible girl. Now why don't you tell Uncle Gerald what it's all about? Confession's good for the soul.' He laughed shortly. 'Or so they say.'

Dorothy glanced at him quickly, but his eyes were on the road, his hands steady on the wheel. He was driving with his usual expertise, concentrating as if he were in a stream of traffic in Regent Street instead of driving down a narrow street with no other cars in sight. Signalling right, he turned into the wide street of Victorian houses, the odd one here and there with striped sun-blinds flapping over closed front doors.

'We're going the wrong way.' Dorothy sat up straight in the low seat, the aftermath of shock at her mother's behaviour leaving her . . . Leaving her with every single nerve in her body alive and quivering. 'This isn't the way home, Gerald. You should have turned left, not right.'

But he made no sign of having heard her, just drove on, away from the west side of the park, away from the wide avenues of red-brick houses, along the almost deserted street. Past a piece of spare land with a group of boys kicking a tin can around, dribbling it from one to another, calling out to each other in high excited voices.

'Get tha skates on, slowcoach!'

'Give us a chance!'

Dorothy stared at them, wondering what would happen if she called out and screamed for help, then she glanced quickly at the set profile of the man at the wheel. Oh, God, but she was the chump to end all chumps . . . She was the character in the play, who, alone and undefended, went off quite willingly with the prime suspect in a murder case. The stupid character at the end of a novel, who, in the last chapter, took a calculated risk, putting herself in the hands of the villain, as if she alone could solve the mystery. How many times had she groaned and put her library book aside, or switched off the wireless, snorting with disgust? And now, she, of her own volition, had got into a car with a man who, she was sure, knew that she knew far more than was good for her. . . .

She shivered and clung on to the sides of her seat as the car, coming to the end of the made-up road, bumped and jerked along a rutted path, with a patchwork of allotments stretching away upwards to the left, and a stubbled field on the right sloping down to the deserted playground of a council school.

And beyond the school, the sprawling panorama of the town: row upon row of terraced houses, with pepper-pot chimneys, curling in curving lines to the cluster of tall mill chimneys pointing sooty fingers up into the clear blue sky. Dorothy turned her head and saw, across the allotments, a long way ahead, the spiral of yellow smoke from a lone bonfire.

'Where do you think you're going?' Her voice trembled

on the verge of lost control. 'There's nothing at the end of
here but an old quarry – Bill Foot's Delph . . .' Her hand
covered her mouth to stifle a scream as she visualized the
derelict place, supposed to be haunted, the place where,
years ago, a tormented man had hurled himself to oblivion.

'Well, Dorothy?' Gerald suddenly, with a squeal of
brakes, brought the red car to a halt by the side of a
hen-run, where a cluster of white and scrawny hens,
separated from them by a tall wire-mesh fence, bobbed and
scratched feverishly at the brown and dusty earth.

'Well, Dorothy?' Gerald took his hands from the wheel as
slowly and lovingly as a concert pianist finishing a
concerto. 'Don't you think it's time you told me what this is
all about?'

Already the sun had deepened his fair skin to pink, and
the wind had tossed the red quiff of hair from its sculptured
perfection so that it lay untidily across his wide forehead.
He turned his wet and enquiring gaze full upon her, wide-
eyed and questioning, and even in that moment of appre-
hension she wondered how her sister Margaret could
possibly find this man attractive? To her he was repulsive,
both in looks and manner, nauseatingly repulsive, and
never more than at that minute.

He was staring bulging eyed at her, holding her glance
with his own, willing her to speak out, daring her to keep
silent, their mutual dislike flaring like a living flame
between them.

And suddenly Dorothy's fear left her, and rage rose up in
her throat, almost choking her. Suddenly, with a flash of
intuition, she knew that this man was the one afraid, not
her . . . this man who had come unbidden into their lives,
wheedling his way into her father's respect, flattering her
foolish, snobbish mother into total subjection, and stealing
Margaret's heart. Placid, trusting Margaret, who would
have believed that black was white, if someone said it firmly
enough.

Their eyes were holding hard. It was a moment of recognition, of putting their cards face down on the ruddy table, as Grandpa Bolton would surely have said. And Dorothy knew what she must do.

Putting her hand into her blazer pocket, she took out the cuff-link and held it out to him on the palm of her hand, not speaking, just holding it out to him, her eyes still steady on his face.

He shook his head, bowed it low, then lifted it sharply, the pale eyes narrowing into threatening slits. 'Where in the name of God did you find it? Tell me, you little interfering sod. Tell me where you found it?'

And as he snatched it from her, hurling it away from him, so that it cleared the wire-mesh fence, falling amongst the hens who fell upon it with a wild flapping of wings, Dorothy knew that he thought it was the *other* one. The cuff-link he had lost that rainswept night in the park, and had been searching for ever since. . . .

And with the realization came the knowledge that she was looking on the panic-stricken face of Ruby Armstrong's killer.

There was a fierce heat welling up inside her, coursing through her body and showing itself in tiny beads of sweat on her upper lip. Her teeth were clenched as she said, 'You did it! You killed that poor girl, and then you dragged her underneath the rhododendron bush and left her lying there. And you went back home, and you went to bed, and you came to our house and you sat at the table and you ate, and you took Margaret to the pictures, and you smiled and smiled . . .' She was shaking now, clenching her fists to stop herself from raking her finger-nails down his shiny pink cheeks. 'And you thought you'd have got away with it. Oh, my God!' She shook her head slowly from side to side. 'And you'd have married Margaret. Married her with that on your mind . . .'

She was so consumed with the power of her anger that even when he stretched out a hand towards her, she felt no fear, merely drew back from him with a look of such loathing on her face that he was the one to recoil.

For the space of a few seconds they stared at each other, then his hand shot out and gripped her round the wrist, in an iron grip that made her cry aloud. 'Right,' he said, snapping out the word. 'Right. Now the cards are on the table, Dorothy. And I suppose you told her big brother what you found out? I suppose you told your precious dad? Was that why you were walking down Steep Brow with a face like an accident going somewhere to happen?'

'No! You're wrong! I told no one.' She tried to wriggle free, but his grip tightened. 'I was running away . . .' Her mind was working frantically. 'I was running away because my mother had found out that Stanley came to the house last night when they were out. She said some dreadful things, and I just walked out. I've done that before when my mother and me have rowed,' she added with desperation.

'Right!' he said again, then before she could move to scramble from the car he had started the engine. Driving on, caring nothing once again for the springs of his beloved car, driving over the rutted road, his foot pressed down hard on the accelerator.

There was murder in his eyes, murder in the way he wrenched at the wheel. This man had killed once, and Dorothy knew that he would have no compunction in killing again. She screamed, and the sound was torn from her throat and tossed away in the slip-stream of onrushing wind.

She fumbled for the door handle, but his hand came out and held her fast.

'No!' she shouted. 'I haven't told anyone! No one, Gerald. Believe me . . .'

But Gerald Tomlin was past believing anything. The temper that had got him into one serious scrape after another all his life, the temper that had caused him to reach out and choke the life out of Ruby Armstrong, was burning him with its all-consuming fire. And this girl, this slip of a girl by his side had taken his shining future in her hands and destroyed it . . . as he would destroy her.

On two wheels the red car turned the corner and roared up the unmade road to Bill Foot's Delph. And in front of them a grassy bank sloped down to the quarry. Stopping with a squeal of brakes, Gerald reached over Dorothy, opened the door and pushed her out, sure that in her state of terror she would be an easy victim for what he planned to do.

But fear had made Dorothy strong, and instead of paralysing her, it lent wings to her feet as she ran towards the quarry, and not away from it as he had expected her to do. Her mind working feverishly she calculated that, if she could crawl beneath the flimsy railing erected not ten yards away from the edge of the sheer drop, she could make her way round to the other side, and if she could climb the grassy bank there, reach the houses seen as a row of chimneys deep in the hollow.

Then she heard a sound behind her that seemed to freeze the very marrow in her bones. The revving of an engine as Gerald drove the car straight for her. . . .

Sure of his undoubted expertise in driving the red car, Gerald was confident enough to take a calculated risk. Sure that after he had run her down he could swerve away from the brink. . . .

With all the strength at her command, Dorothy took a flying leap to land face downwards in the long grass, as Gerald missed her by a fraction of an inch, careering on, for once in his life, the *last* time in his life, misjudging his distance, so that the car, skidding out of control, plunged over the edge of the quarry, turning over and over, bouncing down to the bottom, where it burst into flames.

And it was Mr Crawley who found her, stumbling along the pitted road at the side of the allotments, her face dirty and streaked with tears, her yellow hair falling round her face. Mr Crawley, going home quietly after damping down his fire, to his Sunday dinner after a blissful morning with his pigeons, holding them tenderly in his hands, like the child he had never had, soothing, ringing, spreading their wings wide as he talked to them.

'Nay, lass,' he said. 'Nowt's worth crying like that for, nowt in this silly old world . . .'

And it was Mr Crawley's arms that came round her as she gasped out what had happened, incoherent, pointing back up the hill, shaking, sobbing, trying to make him understand.

And when she had finished he took off his old tweed cap, scratched his head, then put it back again.

'Now tell me where tha' lives, lass, and I'll take thee home,' he said.

Before the afternoon was over, the clouds had formed, the sun had gone, and it was raining hard. As though the bright sunshine of the morning had never been.

Dorothy sat with her father and Margaret in a side room off the women's surgical ward in the infirmary, staring at her mother who lay unmoving and unseeing in the high white bed.

There was nothing they could do. Nothing it seemed that they would ever be able to do ever again for Phyllis Bolton – the Phyllis Bolton they'd always known.

'I want it straight,' Matthew had told the Senior Consultant, a greying man with tired eyes. 'I can cope with the truth, tha knows, so none of tha soft soap, if tha doesn't mind.'

'She's suffered a massive stroke,' the doctor had said, pulling no punches as the broad-shouldered man standing squarely before him had requested. 'She'll never walk again, or speak again. The most you can hope for is some slight movement in her right foot . . . unless there's a miracle.'

'Don't believe in them,' Matthew said, and thanked the

doctor for his frankness, before going back to join his daughters in their bedside vigil.

'I'll stay at home and help to look after her,' Dorothy promised, and what could have passed for a smile crossed Matthew's face. He leaned over and patted her hand.

'I know tha will, chuck,' he said, and knowing this younger child of his even better than he knew himself, he realized that at that very moment she meant it. She were made of good stuff, his Dorothy. He shuddered when he thought how nearly he might have lost her. Felt again the upsurge of relief when, with Arnold driving his car like a maniac, they had found that funny little chap walking along Marston Road with his arm round Dorothy.

'She's had a bit of a shock, gaffer,' Mr Crawley had said, and Matthew, even as he clasped her in his arms, had felt that must surely be the understatement of the year.

Aye, his Dorothy would be all right, and now weren't the time to tell her that he would never allow her to sacrifice herself for the left-over life that this speechless, vegetable of a woman had in front of her. . . .

Poor Phyllis. And poor Margaret. Matthew saw that she was still crying softly into a screwed-up handkerchief, her eyes swollen to narrow slits, and her face puffy and red.

'I want to die!' she had screamed when the ambulance had taken her mother away and he'd had to break the news to her about Gerald. 'I want to die. Oh, Daddy, let me die . . .'

She hadn't called him Daddy for a long time, this un-complicated daughter of his, and somehow it touched him more than her flowing tears and anguished cries. She wouldn't forget this day, not for the rest of her life, but he knew, he knew as sure as the sun would rise on the morrow that, given time, his Margaret would survive. It were the other one . . . Matthew patted Dorothy's hand again. Aye, things went deep with her. . . .

'We'd best be going,' he said. 'There's nowt we can do here.'

And with a backward glance at the still figure on the bed, they walked together down the long stone corridor with its garden-fence-green walls, out of the infirmary to where the black car was parked.

And as they drove into the circular drive and saw Stanley Armstrong waiting patiently in the porch, sheltering from the rain, Matthew whispered to Dorothy to get her sister up to bed.

'I'll have a word with the lad,' he said.

Margaret, still weeping, allowed Dorothy to help her to undress, protesting that she didn't want to live, turning a ravaged face into her pillow, and holding out a wavering hand for another handkerchief.

'How can I ever go out again?' she wailed. 'I'll never go out again. I'll stay in the house and never face people again.'

Dorothy tucked her in, saw that already her poor swollen eyelids were drooping and, closing the door softly behind her, ran downstairs.

The telephone was ringing as she reached the hall, and she told a stuttering Edwin Birtwistle, the captain of the local tennis club for three consecutive seasons, that his kindness in ringing was appreciated. That she quite understood he felt he must get in touch, and that Margaret was taking it all as well as could be expected.

'Tell her that all her friends are standing by her,' he said, and as Matthew came out of the sitting-room Dorothy put a finger to her lips and glanced back upstairs.

Matthew nodded, then pulled a wry face. 'Bad news travels fast, chuck,' he said. 'Go and have a word with him – he's waiting in there.'

'I had to get in touch,' Stanley said, just as Edwin Birtwistle had said. 'Mr Crawley came over with Mrs Crawley. Oh, Dorothy . . .' He stretched out a hand and drew her to him. 'What can I say? I'll never be able to forgive myself for not . . . for not . . .'

Dorothy was so tired that even the effort of forming her mouth round the words was too much of an effort for her. She leaned against him, feeling her legs grow weak beneath her.

'You know about my mother?' she whispered.

He stroked her hair. 'Your father's just told me. It's awful . . . oh God, can anything else happen? It's all so awful!'

Then, as they sat together on the chesterfield, he told her that Matthew had told him that he was making his mother an allowance so that he could take up his scholarship to Oxford.

'In the middle of all this he told me that,' he said, shaking his head. 'He's a wonderful man, your father.'

And strangely enough there was nothing more to say . . . and so they just sat there, with the rain pouring down the window panes, and when he got up to go Dorothy walked with him to the door, and stood there until he had walked away, turning the corner out of sight. Tall, falling over his feet, head bent, the rain beating down on his thin shoulders.

She found her father sitting at the kitchen table, his hands clasped together on its scrubbed surface, sitting there as if he was wondering what to do.

Dorothy went to him and leaned her cheek against his thinning hair. 'That was a nice thing you told Stanley,' she said softly. 'Now he won't go making any dramatic statements after the funeral tomorrow about giving up his scholarship. That's what he intended to do, you know.'

Matthew nodded. 'I guessed as much. In fact he told me as much. He's a grand lad, chuck.'

Dorothy moved round and went to sit opposite to her father at the big table. And the house was quiet around them, with only the steady drip of the rain outside to break the silence.

'Aye, a grand lad,' Matthew said again.

Dorothy saw the way his features were blurred into unfamiliar lines with exhaustion and the sadness of the day. Some day she'd tell him that what had been between her and Stanley was all over. Perhaps she'd even try to explain how her love for him had died at the moment she had taken his jacket from him and hung it up in the hall.

'Love can die at the most unexpected moment, the most mundane moment,' she would say. 'How can that be? Tell me how that can be?'

And even her beloved father, in his infinite wisdom, wouldn't be expected to understand. . . .

But she was wrong. For Matthew Bolton, aged at least five years in the space of an afternoon, and tired beyond sleep, would have understood perfectly.

How could the love of so many years have died in a single second, he was asking himself silently at that very moment? How could he have looked at Phyllis as she lashed out with her fist at Dorothy and known that never, for as long as he lived, would he feel the same way about her again?

Look after her he would. Cherish what was left of her for always, without question, but something in him had died and would never be restored.

'Thank God there'll be no trial and all the muck-raking that would have entailed,' he said at last, as if they were continuing a conversation, and as if at an unspoken command they reached across the table and clasped hands.

'It'll be reet, lass,' Matthew Bolton said. 'Things usually turn out reet in the end.'

'You sound just like Grandpa Bolton,' Dorothy said, and as she saw the way the tears sprang to his eyes, she got up quickly and, moving over to the gas-stove, put the kettle on.

'A cup of tea?' she asked, being careful not to turn round.

On the following pages are some of Marie Joseph's latest best-selling titles, also published by Arrow.

A LEAF IN THE WIND

Marie Joseph

She was hardship's child – born to struggle and to serve.

He was fortune's favourite – born to flourish and be served.

They lived worlds apart. Jenny was the girl from the cat-meat shop, born into squalor and defeat. Paul Tunstall was a soldier and a gentleman, arrogant and charming, with his silver-light eyes and boyish smile. And yet from the moment they met there was a spark between them – and their separate lives of pain and loneliness seemed to beckon to each other.

But should she succumb to that plea in his eyes, to that longing in herself? Should she cross the line of class, the boundaries of propriety? Dare Jenny risk all to lose herself to love?

£1.50